Christopher Evans was born in
Capella's Golden Eyes, The Ins
co-editor with Robert Holdstock
an
and lives in London.

WIGAN LIBRARIES
WITHDRAWN FOR
BOOK SALE

31. OCT

85066137

By the same author

Capella's Golden Eyes
The Insider
In Limbo

CHRISTOPHER EVANS

Chimeras

Grafton
An Imprint of HarperCollinsPublishers

Grafton
An Imprint of HarperCollins*Publishers*
77–85 Fulham Palace Road,
Hammersmith, London W6 8JB

A Grafton Original 1992
9 8 7 6 5 4 3 2 1

Copyright © Christopher Evans 1992

The Author asserts the moral right to
be identified as the author of this work

A catalogue record for this book
is available from the British Library

ISBN 0 586 21304 X

Set in Times

Printed in Great Britain by
HarperCollinsManufacturing Glasgow

703237

All rights reserved. No part of this publication may be
reproduced, stored in a retrieval system, or transmitted,
in any form or by any means, electronic, mechanical,
photocopying, recording or otherwise, without the prior
permission of the publishers.

This book is sold subject to the condition that it shall not,
by way of trade or otherwise, be lent, re-sold, hired out or
otherwise circulated without the publisher's prior consent
in any form of binding or cover other than that in which it
is published and without a similar condition including this
condition being imposed on the subsequent purchaser.

To
Writers' Bloc
who saw it happen.

1

Transmutations

Damn that boy! Where was he?

Shubi surfaced from a muddled dream to the stillness and silence of her room. Grey morning light leaked through the gaps in the window blind.

She pushed herself up on her elbows, still thinking about the boy, all too conscious that he was long gone from her life. There was a damp patch where she had been lying – she'd wet herself again!

Up you get, old woman. The bed creaked as she heaved herself off it, a horrible wheeze escaping from the depths of her throat. She stumbled to the window, pulled the blind.

The sun was hidden behind the clutter of terracotta roofs. Down below in the courtyard a brindled dog sniffed among a scattering of rotten tomatoes, avocado rinds, bread husks and eggshells. The morning air was chill, the cobbles slick with dew. She heard someone calling her, the words coming from afar, from long ago . . .

'Shubi! Shubi!'

Two voices, shouting as one. The twins, Jenna and Neresh.

'I'm here!' she cried.

They came scurrying through the grove, ducking under the boughs and finding her in her usual place, in the hollow next to the irrigation channel. Here it was shady, and they were safe from prying adult eyes.

They sat down at her feet, girl and boy, alike as two peas. Brown-skinned, black hair cut short, both of them dressed in bleached cotton tunics. They were her disciples, which was only fitting because they were just eight and she was ten.

'We're ready,' Jenna said eagerly, her brown eyes bright.

Shubi played innocent. 'For what?'

'The spirits, of course. What are you going to make for us today?'

'Have you brought me anything?'

5

Neresh delved into his trouser pocket and produced three sticks of liquorice which he hastily straightened. Shubi pocketed them ceremoniously, then nodded. Nothing pleased her more than fashioning the spirits; she would have done it without reward, but already she knew that pleasures paid for are more valued than those given free.

'No one followed you?' she asked.

'No one,' they both assured her.

But it always paid to check. She climbed up on the boundary wall, peering over the tops of the orange trees. They stretched in all directions, filling the shallow valley, row after row of glossy green leaves dotted with pale blossom and bright fruit. Between the lines of trees she could see other children, diligently hoeing and weeding. The fruit would not be ripe for another month or two, but there was always work to be done, always drudgery. The adults were busy planting saplings in the new groves higher up the valley sides.

She clambered down, satisfied that no one else was near. Already she could feel the spirits gathering like ripples in the air, soft insistent breezes. She had always been able to sense them, far more strongly than anyone else she knew. The few adults who also felt their presence simply ignored them, and children were taught to do the same. But she, alone one evening in the fields, had suddenly had an image of an awesome and terrifying white bird descending from the sky. Something rushed through her mind, and she saw to her amazement the same white bird flicker into existence right in front of her eyes as a shiver overtook her. She'd transformed a spirit into the picture that was in her head.

Of course the bird had been small and ill-formed, and it immediately dropped to earth, bursting into a greyish dust. But that night, while her brothers and sisters slept, she'd experimented again, letting the spirits flood her mind before concentrating on an insect, one of the black weevils from the fields. Something dropped on her blanket, and she saw the weevil sitting there before she crushed it to powder in her fright.

'What are you going to show us?' Neresh asked impatiently.

'Be quiet,' she said, closing her eyes and concentrating.

There were any number of things. Recently she'd created

6

chessboard pieces in bright primary colours, none bigger than the palm of her hand, all soon turning grey and falling apart when they were handled. But she was getting better, the colours brighter and the shapes lasting longer each time.

'What are you thinking of?' Jenna whispered.

'SSSHHH!'

The spirits were all around her now, pressing in on the edges of her mind. They had no thoughts – they were just presences, urgent to be brought forth into the real world in whatever shape she wanted. All she had to do was squeeze them out with her mind.

She stretched out her arms, palms upturned, and felt their heady rush. Dimly she heard Jenna give a whoop of joy.

She knew they were there before she opened her eyes; she could feel them resting on her palms. Both balls were identical, emerald green blotched with crimson.

She offered them to the twins. If anything, they looked disappointed, not appreciating that she had never until now managed to give her creations more than a single flat colour.

Neresh took his ball and flung it casually into the air. It fell to the baked earth, exploding into an ashen cloud.

Shubi was furious.

'Give me that one back!' she said to Jenna, whose ball was already losing its colour.

She tried to snatch it from her. There was a brief struggle before the ball disintegrated between their hands.

'Witch!' Neresh shrieked. 'You're a witch!'

And he and his sister ran off through the trees.

Squatting over the bowl, she relieved herself. As usual, her hip ached abominably. Where had she put her damned stick?

She had turned the mirror above the washbasin to the wall, unable to bear the sight of her face. Everything was turning yellow – teeth, eyes, skin, even her grey rats'-tails hair. She looked like the sort of hag who terrified young children.

The kettle began to sing on the hotplate. She found the stick propped up against the bottom of the bed. On the wall she'd hung a calendar, and she saw that she'd ringed one of the days. That was it! That was why she'd been dreaming about the boy. Today was the opening of the exhibition.

She began scuttling about the room, wondering what she should wear. Not her cloak, even though it was the warmest thing she had; he'd recognize her easily in that. She wanted to be invisible, just part of the crowd. What then? Think, woman, think! Her long grey undergown that buttoned up from crotch to neck. The linen dress with the long skirt. Her black woollen leggings and canvas boots. And a coat? Where was the black serge one with the big collar?

Shubi! Shubi!

Stop yelling, damn you! She sat down heavily on the edge of the bed, her chest creaking like a badly hung door. If there had been anyone else in the room she would never have believed the noise was coming from her. Still the calling went on.

'Shubi! Shubi!'

Her father's voice, carrying fierce and strong from the village square above the swirling sounds of harmonica and fiddle.

Jered immediately pulled back, but she clutched him to her again.

'Don't stop now!' she whispered urgently.

He had been covering her neck with kisses, and she had bared a breast so that he could fondle it. He swallowed, looked anxious as her father shouted her name again.

'He won't find us here,' she assured him.

They were on the blind side of old Ruash's barn, rampant white-flowered bushes in the wasteground shielding them. She pressed her back against an inward-sloping wall, drinking in the musky scent of the blossoms.

'Shubi! Shubi!'

The shouts were fainter, drowned by the music. Her father was heading off in the other direction.

Reassured, Jered resumed his kissing and fondling. She pushed a knee between his legs, holding him tight to her, her mind elsewhere entirely. Her parents had found the statuette of the woman with the parasol – a stony figure that she had fashioned from the air only days before. It was her best creation so far, and when it first emerged the woman had been gaily dressed in scarlet and cream, her parasol matching. Even after the colours faded, she'd been unable to bring herself to dispose of it and had kept it under her pillow. Her mother had found it while changing the sheets.

Jered breathed heavily in her ear and kneaded her breast as if searching for something inside it. Shubi stroked his back, urged him on. She hoped she was doing it right. Sixteen, and she'd hardly ever been kissed until now. Time she took affairs into her own hands.

Of course her father had been furious. He was always making her promise to 'stop conjuring those damned essences', as he called them, and she was always breaking her promise. They wouldn't leave her alone, and she couldn't leave them alone. 'We're farmers,' he would tell her, 'workers with our hands', but the fields bored her, always had. This latest act of defiance had been the final straw for him. She was of an age now, and he'd announced that he was going to marry her off. He'd visited Malakot to arrange the examination which would establish her virginity before she was put up for marriage.

Well, Malakot would have a surprise because she wasn't going to be a virgin much longer. As soon as she knew of her father's intentions, she'd sought out Jered, who was always boasting of his conquests. She cared little for him, but he was handsome enough and about the same age as herself. When she'd asked him to meet her behind the barn at dusk he'd looked at her, amazed. Then he'd shrugged and said he'd think about it. But he was waiting for her when she arrived.

Heavenly host, all this kissing was an ordeal! Her lips felt bruised from Jered's gobbling. The carnival music swirled down from the square, and she could sense the spirits coming closer.

She supposed she was ready, though it was hard to tell whether she felt aroused or just impatient. She twisted her mouth away from his.

'Now,' she said. 'Get on with it.'

He merely redoubled his frantic kissing. She coiled both legs around him, pulling him tighter to her. Then she freed her right hand and reached down to unbutton his shorts.

He broke free, lurching backwards, swallowing and shaking his head.

Shubi pulled herself upright. 'What's the matter?'

'Nothing. I'm not ready yet, that's all.'

'What is it? I know I'm not beautiful –'

'It's not that.'

He stared down at his sandalled feet, kicked at a tuft of grass. He was blushing!

She said, 'You've never done it before, have you?'

'Of course I have! I've had dozens of girls.'

'I'm a virgin too.'

'I know *you* are,' he said defiantly. 'I can tell.'

She stood up, brushing bits of hay from her skirt. 'I won't say anything to anyone.'

'I'm going back to watch the carnival.'

She felt like whacking him across the ear.

'Why did you come?'

He tore a tall weed from the ground, flung it away. 'I thought you were going to show me something.'

'Show you something? What?'

'I know what you do. With the presences. Everyone knows.'

So *that* was the forbidden fruit he wanted! She might have known.

The spirits had thickened all around her, only too eager to be brought forth. Suddenly, maliciously, she smiled and said, 'All right. I'll give you what you want.'

She should never have done it, of course; it was mean and cruel. But without pausing to think, she materialized the image that was in her mind, seeing it blink into existence at head-height in the shadowed space. The flood of release exceeded any pleasure Jered could have given her.

Jered gaped when he saw it. He stumbled back as if she had hit him, called her a slut and a whore. Then he turned and ran, hurrying out of sight through a clump of bushes.

Shubi heard herself laughing, but there was little real mirth in it. The erect penis slowly began to sink towards the earth as it lost colour and turned to stone; she had fashioned it so swiftly that it had immediately begun to decay. Whistles and cheers carried from the square. Shubi snatched the floating penis, flung it down, and ground it to dust under her bare heel.

She climbed the alleyway to the square, already feeling trapped. Her father would find her a dull-witted husband who would make her cook his meals and fill the house up with children. All the talk would be of farming, and she would turn into a stupid resentful sow. And as she sank into drudgery, the spirits would abandon her for ever.

The square was filled with villagers and the gay gold and scarlet wagons of the Wanderers. They had arrived the previous morning, and Ruash let them pasture their horses in his fields. Now they were entertaining for their supper. Before her rendezvous with Jered, Shubi had watched a slab of a woman wrestle with a huge green snake, her arms and legs tattooed with reptilian designs so that she appeared at times to merge with the creature. Now an albino girl no older than herself was dancing with three sickly-looking apes and encouraging them to leap through hoops with urgent motions of her hands.

Shubi pushed herself to the front of the crowd just as the dance ended. She envied the girl her freedom and the bright scarves she wore. The Wanderers travelled the whole land in their wagons, and this was their first visit in over a generation. They were swarthy, black-haired folk, and the albino girl scarcely seemed one of them.

Her dance over, the girl offered to tell fortunes by reading palms. A line of villagers swiftly formed beside the seat she had taken, and Shubi was among them. She watched a strongman lift children in a water barrel and pull a cartload of hay across the square with his teeth. She scanned the onlookers' faces for her family, but there was no sign of them. Suddenly it was her turn.

She crouched before the albino and offered her hand. The girl's eyes were as pink as watered blood.

'What's your name?' Shubi asked.

The girl looked surprised. She said, 'Taliko.'

A big woman in crimson robes strode to the centre of the square. Her grey hair flowed down her back, tied with ribbons at its ends. There was something about her that immediately commanded Shubi's attention.

'Who's she?' Shubi asked.

'Rosenna,' Taliko told her. 'She's head of our clan.'

The woman was concentrating in a manner all too familiar to Shubi. Abruptly four white doves exploded from her hands, shooting up into the air and hovering around her head. The birds looked real, their movements perfectly natural. Shubi pulled her hand away from Taliko, scarcely able to believe

11

her eyes. The doves, spirit-creations, hung steadily in the air on beating wings. Shubi had conjured white birds herself, but she had never imagined she could give them movement.

Now the birds descended to settle on a low wall beside the temple. With a dramatic flourish, the woman brought forth a small sailing ship, carefully detailed and coloured, which bobbed through the air, making the onlookers duck as it floated by. Meanwhile the birds on the wall stiffened as their white plumage faded to grey.

Several children scrambled forward to claim the stone doves as prizes. The woman watched their squabbling indulgently, allowing the victors to carry the birds away. The crowd sounded its approval and flung coins into the collection boxes placed around the square.

The ship sailed away down the hill, pursued by a riotous crowd of infants. Rosenna succumbed to a spate of coughing, but she quickly recovered. Then, to Shubi's astonishment, she materialized a life-sized black horse with wings sprouting from its flanks. It reared upward, its hoofs making scrabbling sounds on the cobbles.

Another wonder! Shubi had never managed to fashion anything of such a size. Whenever she tried, her creations simply dissolved away immediately they emerged. The wings were particularly splendid, each twice the span of a man's arms, raising dust as they beat the air.

The woman grasped the animal's mane, obviously intending to mount it. All around the square the crowd roared its appreciation. Shubi was suddenly furious with them. Jumping to her feet, she concentrated hard and summoned forth her own creation – an ape similar to those she had seen earlier, but pure white. She imagined it astride the horse's back, clinging tight to its mane. Her body shuddered as a spirit rushed through her.

And there it was! Rosenna stepped back in surprise. The horse spread its wings and leapt into the air.

Shubi, on thinking of the ape, had willed it to have complete powers of movement, and she was delighted to see it grip the mane and flex its legs tight around the horse's flanks as it rose high above the square, wings beating like sheets flapping in a gale. Up and up it soared before plunging down, the ape clasped to its neck.

The crowd scattered, for it was plain the horse was not going to stop. None of the Wanderers moved apart from the woman, who took a single step back. Shubi was transfixed; despite the danger, she noted that the colour was beginning to fade from both horse and ape as they plummeted down.

They crashed to earth in front of the temple door, scattering debris. Pieces of stone struck her skirt, gritty dust choking her eyes and throat.

She blinked her eyes clear as the dust gradually settled. The woman was still standing there, staring at her. Of the winged horse and the white ape, nothing remained except for fragments of grey rock.

The crowd slowly filtered back into the square. Shubi stepped forward.

'Was the ape yours?' the woman asked.

'Yes,' Shubi said, unable to restrain a proud grin. 'I want to join your clan.'

The woman slapped her so hard across the cheek that she was sent reeling.

The stairs were narrow, with loose boards everywhere. Slowly. Slowly. She leaned heavily on her stick, free hand flat against the wall. Gradually she descended, pausing on each landing to catch her breath. Of course it was worse going up, and old Elula never liked having to visit her. Worse than useless he was, with his bent back and quivering hands. He gave her sleeping draughts which she never took, and told her he couldn't do anything for her unless she had complete rest. 'Then get yourself out of here!' she would yell at him, and if there was a pillow at hand she'd fling it at him, sending him scurrying from the room.

There. Down at last. She limped along the dingy corridor which always stank of dogs. A hat. She'd forgotten to bring a hat. Well, it was too late to go back for it now.

She heaved open the door and shuffled out on to the street. The raw morning air knifed down her throat, making her cough so much that her eyes blurred. Afterwards there was a thin whining sound in her head. That she should have come to this! She used her stick to launch herself off again, thinking back to her youth, to the days of her prime.

* * *

13

'Shubi?'

She spun around as Taliko entered the wagon.

'Hell's bones!' she cried. 'You scared the wits from me.'

Taliko crept forward, squinting in the gloom. 'What are you doing?'

'Packing.' Her canvas pack was spread out on the bunk.

'Why?'

'I'm going to Veridi-Almar to seek my fortune.'

Shubi spoke half-mockingly, but Taliko would know she was in earnest. Through the wagon's doorway the deep blue dusk was pierced by the flames of the funeral fire. Pipe music sounded a fluting anthem to the departed, and the Wanderers were dancing around the fire.

'Veridi-Almar?' Taliko said uncertainly. 'Why there?'

'It's the capital,' Shubi announced, as if it was a fact unknown to her friend. 'There's nothing for me here now that Rosenna's gone.'

Taliko looked stunned, though Shubi was sure she had known it was coming.

'But what about your act?' she said. 'You know it's you they come to see most.'

'You'll manage without me.'

Taliko shook her head. 'You can't go now.'

'I have to.'

'But why?'

'There's every reason. You know that as well as I do.'

For a moment there was silence. Shubi folded a blouse into her bag.

'Are you leaving tonight?' Taliko asked.

'That's the plan.'

'You should never travel alone by night –'

'Or cross flowing water or wear pink,' Shubi mocked. 'Remember when you read my palm? You told me I'd find good fortune if I was bold. I'm following your advice.'

Shubi held out her arms. They embraced.

'Have you told anyone else?' Taliko asked.

'Of course I haven't. They'd try to keep me here, you know that.'

'Don't go. You're my only friend.'

The bond between them had always been strong. Though of

Wanderer stock, Taliko was an orphan, and the oth[..]
to regard her as something of a freak, not really part [..]
clan. As for Shubi herself, she had never been fully accept[..]
despite the fact that she drew more crowds and filled money
boxes faster than anyone else. They were both, in their different
ways, outsiders. But Shubi had already survived a greater loss
when she abandoned her family. Her ties to the Wanderers had
always been looser.

'I have to go,' she said simply. 'I've made up my mind.'

Taliko nibbled at her lower lip and bowed her head. Her hair
looked like silver thread in the lamplight. Abruptly she turned
and hurried out of the wagon.

Outside the music and dancing continued above the crackling
fire. Shubi buckled up her bag and went down the steps. She had
acquired few possessions in her eight years with the Wanderers,
but then she'd had nothing except what she was wearing when
she had stowed away in one of the wagons. By the time she was
found the Wanderers had already left her village far behind.
Rosenna must have let her stay because she was dying and
needed a successor to draw the crowds.

The air was fragrant with smoke and the pines which bordered
their camp. Shubi crept around the corner of a wagon to peer at
the fire.

Flames blazed high and sparks billowed into the darkness as
Elazar the strongman added a big fir branch. Men were dancing
with women, widows with children, babies were bound tight to
their mothers' backs. She knew all their names now, and had
shared her bed with many of the men as the price of her
continued acceptance. Yet just as often the men crept to her
wagon by night not to bed her but to ask for a private creation,
a favoured image, which they would take away hidden under
their cloaks and show to no one.

Cones popped and resin flared orange in the blaze. The
music swirled about her, but she made no move to join the
dance and kept herself hidden. Beyond the fire stood the
dead cork oak in whose spreading branches Rosenna was
laid; embroidered scarves hung from her arms and legs. The
Wanderers believed that the spirits of the air received the souls
of the dead.

Shubi had endured much for the sake of Rosenna's guidance

15

ın the art of fashioning the spirits. She was determined to learn how to give her creations movement, how to make them bigger, brighter, altogether more lifelike. Rosenna gave advice only grudgingly at first, but in the end Shubi won her respect because she persisted against every discouragement. She found it hard to repeat her success with the white ape, but eventually she began to fashion beetles which twitched sluggishly, then butterflies which drifted slowly through the air. Gradually she progressed until she produced piebald bats, mottled eagles, shimmering fairy-like creatures, and finally a winged woman, almost life-sized, golden-skinned and angelic of face, which flew around the wagons for several exhilarating moments before dissolving into a dusty mist.

'It's all in the power of the vision,' Rosenna told her. 'The more strongly you see, the more real the creation. The harder you concentrate on bringing them forth, the longer they'll last.'

This squared with her own experience. Her better creations not only lasted longer but precipitated into a harder stone when they finally lost their colour and mobility. Increasingly she began to observe things more carefully: an owl's flight across the sky at dusk, the patterns of leaves on a hawthorn bush, a smile, the way a crystal vase captured the afternoon sunlight, how reflections were fractured in flowing water. She forced herself to concentrate, holding the spirits at bay and ignoring all distractions, until she was sure that her vision was as clear and vivid as possible before she released it into the world. Frequently she knew she had fashioned something strong by the sheer power of the feelings which washed through her at the instant of creation.

Rosenna only ever offered encouragement in a negative sense. 'One day you might be good,' she would say; or, 'I've seen worse.' But then she began to insist that Shubi help her with her performances 'to lighten the load'; she suffered badly from a chest complaint and frequent breathlessness. Eventually Shubi developed a repertoire which included clouds of fireflies, flurries of mist, acrobatic trolls, and a monstrous fanged head which appeared to swallow both of them before it dissolved away.

As the years passed, Shubi took over more and more of

the performance until finally she began to appear alone. She delighted in the sound of coins showering into the money boxes, in the way she could play on the emotions of the villagers they entertained, in the way they gazed at her with awe and respect afterwards. But Rosenna was always quick to dampen any self-importance. 'You should see the artists in Veridi-Almar,' she would say. 'The things they can do – it would leave you gasping.' While refusing to give details, she managed to portray the capital as a bustling place where there were artists on every street corner. Sometimes Shubi was sure she invented the stories, because the Wanderers were shy of large settlements and never went near any cities. But she yearned to go to the Veridi-Almar of her imagination and compete with the best. At last the time had come.

The Wanderers were now dancing around the oak, brandishing torches lit from the fire. Rosenna had died the previous night, leaving no instructions to the clan. Fat Velanca the Snakewoman had been chosen as her successor, and there was no love lost between her and Shubi. It was Velanca who now stepped forward to light the ends of Rosenna's scarves.

The flames raced rapidly upwards. Shubi turned away, heading off towards the dusty road along which they had travelled the previous morning. Veridi-Almar was six or seven days' walk to the south, and she had hoarded enough money to give herself a start in the city, come what may.

As she hurried past an outlying wagon, a figure stepped out, startling her. But it was only Taliko.

'That's the second time in a single evening!' Shubi said.

'You can't go,' Taliko whispered with great urgency. 'I've consulted the cards, and your journey isn't favoured.'

Taliko's life was ruled by superstition: it had made her timid. Shubi sighed and shook her head.

'It's favoured by me,' she said.

'If you travel alone, you risk death.'

She looked utterly serious, though Shubi was certain she was making it up as a desperate measure.

'Taliko,' she said softly, 'I'm going.'

'Then you mustn't travel alone.'

17

Taliko reached behind the wagon and hauled out a travelling bag of her own. From her pocket she withdrew the silvery egg-shaped stone which was her favourite good-luck charm.

'This will help us travel safely,' she said excitedly.

A thin mist shrouded the waterfront. Was it early? She'd seen no one since setting out. The Raimus lapped grey against the bank.

Many of the riverside warehouses had been demolished during the summer, and two huge stone columns rose out of the muddy black earth. As usual, no one knew what was happening, but according to rumour the Hierarch was having a great bridge built to span the Raimus, permanently linking the two halves of the capital.

A ferry rested against one of the wharves, its shallow hold filled with sacks of grain. The ferryman was about to cast off. Shubi hobbled up to him.

'I need passage across,' she announced.

'I'm full,' the ferryman said without looking up. 'Find someone else.'

'I'll perish if I have to stand here! Have you no sympathy for an old woman?'

The ferryman was young. Something told her he had a kindly nature.

'I've no money,' she said. 'My sister's dying, and she needs me.'

His eyes narrowed. 'She must be rich if she lives across the river.'

'She's a servant!' Shubi snapped, mustering both irritation and outrage. She added a brief spasm of coughing, leaning heavily on her stick.

The ferryman reached out both hands to help her on board, found her a place between two snugly enfolding grainsacks.

They cast off, and the ferryman quickly became absorbed in manipulating the rudders. What a rogue she was! Inventing dying sisters and not even offering him a single coin from her purse! She chuckled to herself. One of the few benefits of age was that it allowed you to take advantage of the young.

The mist began to lift as the ferry crossed the river. She thought she felt a breeze on the back of her head, then realized it was an inquisitive spirit. She shooed it away, deliberately blanking her thoughts. Still they tried to come, those damned spirits, even though she was all used up. They pestered her like mosquitoes, like whispered gossip that she didn't want to hear.

'Shubi?'

She looked up from her hoeing, saw no one. Then Sephea emerged from the shadows, ducking her head under the overhanging vine. She picked her way through the rows of onions and tomatoes.

'There's laundry to be delivered,' she said to Shubi. 'Will you take it?'

Shubi nodded, relieved to be spared further work in the garden on such a hot day.

'Thank you,' Sephea said. 'The mule's waiting outside.'

'I'll be along shortly.'

Sephea nodded and withdrew, her deep blue skirt dragging in the dusty earth.

Resting on her hoe, Shubi wiped sweat from her forehead with the back of her hand. High above, swifts swooped and glided, black darts against the blue. She liked the quietness of the garden, the sense of security provided by the stone walls which enclosed it. It was over a year since her arrival at the retreat, and only recently had she begun venturing out into the city on errands.

The hooded dark blue cloak was a gift from the Comforters. Draping it over her shoulder, she limped out of the garden and went down a cool stone corridor to one of the outer doors.

The mule was tethered to a post outside, a wicker basket strapped to its back. It was a docile beast, slow but uncomplaining. She unleashed it, led it out through the main gate.

On the street it always seemed hotter, flies buzzing everywhere, the rampant smells of the tumbledown city assailing her. Veridi-Almar was a maze of narrow winding streets and alleyways. The buildings seemed to have been thrown up with great haste, level upon level, in an entirely disorganized manner. Arcs of washing hung from windows, baskets of wilting flowers stood on ledges, palms and bright-flowered creepers on the balconies of the better-off houses. Only in the broader

19

avenues and parks did the city seem to retreat momentarily, to allow a breathing-space. She wondered what Taliko would have made of it.

There were few people about, for it was still early, and she welcomed the relative quiet. Sometimes she was asked to visit the market, always something of an ordeal because the people here were inveterate bargainers who expected a customer to haggle, whether over a silver necklace or a humble turnip.

Taliko had never reached Veridi-Almar. On their last night, in sight of the city, they made the mistake of sleeping in an open field instead of finding lodgings. To this day, Shubi was certain the men had come from the village they visited the night before, and she blamed herself for an over-ostentatious display of her talents in the resthouse where they stayed. Her creations were too vivid and entertaining, filling their purses. Greedy eyes must have been watching, and they must have been followed and attacked while they slept.

Even now she recalled only flashes of what happened in the aftermath. She woke in the back of a hay-cart bouncing its way along a rutted lane. The pain in her hip was such agony that she knew it was broken. Taliko lay alongside her with open eyes and a bloody mouth. She was quite dead, though her head kept lolling towards Shubi's face with every jounce of the cart, as if seeking a kiss. Never had Shubi felt such grief, such paralysing terror. Then blackness claimed her once more.

When next she woke she was in a bed in a cool stone room, safe in a Comforters' retreat. Those who tended her were softly spoken and kind, feeding her soup and cleaning the wounds on her limbs and body. Day upon sunlit day passed, and she recovered only slowly. But gradually her hip began to heal and the Comforters would take her for halting walks around the garden. There were others in their charge, men and women too sick or poor or old to fend for themselves.

She met the man who had saved her, an old farmer who possessed nothing except compassion. He quivered with embarrassment when she thanked him. The retreat lay in the heart of the city, but for a long time she had no interest in what was beyond its formidable stone walls. But finally, when her health returned and she was able to walk without pain, she offered to

20

work in the vegetable garden and run errands for the Comforters to repay her debt to them.

The laundry was situated at the end of a street filled with market stalls. Shubi exchanged the basket of dirty linen for one containing freshly laundered clothes. Afterwards she paused at a stall to admire a pair of leather sandals. The woman at the stall tried to press them into her hands, but Shubi shook her head, retreating. She had no money, was entirely dependent on the Comforters' charity.

Unexpectedly, she felt a stirring in her mind, and peered across the street. Standing under an awning was a young man, his eyes closed in concentration. A small crowd was watching him. Shubi immediately knew he was a street artist preparing to perform for passersby. More strongly now, she could sense the presence of the spirits. Chimeras, they called them here, fanciful products of the mind. She felt as if they were trying to murmur secrets to her.

She hobbled on, pulling the mule after her, deliberately turning away from the man. She had avoided seeing any other artists' work since arriving in the city. It was hard enough keeping her own spirits at bay; they were becoming more insistent now that her strength was returning.

At a trickling fountain, Shubi stopped to take a drink, her head alive with a soft babbling. In front of her a yellow-and-green lizard was sunning itself on a whitewashed wall. Suddenly, with a rush and a flurry, a spirit surged through her, and instantly a replica of the lizard appeared under the water of the fountain bowl.

It was poorly formed, a crude imitation of the original, and entirely without movement. She was both shocked and thrilled by it. The abrupt rush had startled her, unlocked a memory of Taliko displaying her good-luck stone at the resthouse, a memory of one of their attackers crying: 'The stone! Find the stone!' They had thought the worthless piece of rock valuable, and Taliko had died because of it.

Shubi straightened from the fountain, tears running down her cheeks. It was a moment before she could steady herself. Tugging at the mule's harness, she set off again with greater determination than before. She would return to the retreat and tell the Comforters that at last she was ready to leave.

More spirits gathered as she pushed her way through the crowds. Invisible, immaterial, they were nevertheless as restless and as real as the people who jostled her, who cursed or protested at her lumbering mule. Her mind was filled with images of Taliko – reading her palm, sharing supper with her, soaping her back, falling asleep with her head in her lap. The spirits' urgency increased, forcing her to resist them. She wanted to give herself proper pause to imagine Taliko in some favoured setting which she would reproduce as a miniature still-life, an object of memory and affection and renewal.

Panting and wheezing, she mounted the steps of the jetty and set off down the well-heeled streets where the houses of the rich and the nobility were concentrated. Here there were no scavenging dogs, no slops and dung stinking in open ditches, just clean cobbled streets and imposing stuccoed buildings huddled around inner courtyards and gardens, presenting blank walls to the outside world.

And there it was at last: Lord Orizay's town house, a castellated mansion set at the end of an avenue of beech trees.

A cluster of people were already waiting outside the entrance, and an atmosphere of restrained expectation prevailed. There was much talk of the artist's work, of his remarkable gifts. Among the crowd were people she judged as merchants and officials and perhaps even a minor lord or two; but many were commoners like herself. This pleased her, though she wondered if they would all be allowed in. As far as she knew, the exhibition was free, but it was entirely possible that they would have to pay to get in. She had a handful of coins in her purse and, if necessary, she would surrender them all.

A sudden breeze made her shudder, and set the dry golden leaves whispering . . .

'Shubi.'

He hissed the word out, as if he didn't like its sound. He was tall and lean, dressed entirely in black.

'I'm Ophre,' he told her. 'Are you sure you've got no money?'

He was still holding out his box. She shook her head.

'I'd pay you if I could. I really liked what you fashioned.'

The rest of the crowd were already melting away from the park. Ophre made a noncommittal sound, as if compliments meant nothing to him. But Shubi truly never had seen anything quite like his display – the cavorting group of obscenely caricatured lords and ladies, crudely formed but possessed with considerable powers of movement. Ophre had portrayed them as cannibals at a grotesque feast, eating the lavishly dressed bodies of poor folk, roasted and garnished on silver platters. The whole scene, only just smaller than life-size, had dissolved to nothingness a few moments before several soldiers marched into the park.

Ophre squinted at her. 'You're not from the city.'

Shubi shook her head, told him the name of her village.

'Are you an artist yourself?'

'I –' She was surprised he appeared to have divined this. 'I used to be.'

'Used to be? Is it something you cast away, like an old vest?'

She didn't know if she could explain. The soldiers were still lingering nearby, eyeing them. Ophre reached under her cloak and took her wrist.

'Come,' he said. 'You can tell me about it over a cup of wine.'

But he got the story out of her as they walked along together, Shubi struggling with her limp to keep up with him.

On leaving the retreat, she found work in the laundry, renting a room above it. In the evenings, alone in her room, she began fashioning the spirits again, producing tiny boats, houses, animals and people seen on the streets – dull, unambitious art, but necessary practice after a year of neglect. Then she visited an official exhibition of works by some of the city's most respected artists, housed in a big marble building close to the Hierarch's palace. She had emerged feeling crushed.

What a fool she was to have imagined she could compete with the élite! Wandering around the great halls, staring at the creations mounted on pedestals or free-floating in spaces of their own, she felt awed and dismayed. The artists had created not single figures or objects or even groups of them, but whole environments. She wandered from one to another, agog. On a raft-like mount, fleets of ships engaged on a stormy sea; overhead, angels and devils were at war in a blood-red inferno.

Size was not the object, she understood that, because none of the tableaux was larger than a tabletop. She peered closely at a fortress under siege. Evidently movement and fine attention to detail were also considered unnecessary; this scene, like all the others, was a still-life, the individual soldiers mere smears of colour, the violence compressed into a single frozen moment by swirls and stipples of light and shade.

To think that she had been so proud of her creations, her diminutive figures, her ersatz birds and beasts, her pale and stilted reflections of the city and the countryside. Compared to the exhibition works they were paltry in their ambition, crude in their execution, mere child's play.

For days afterwards she abandoned all her fashioning, working long hours in the steaming laundry before retreating to her room where she brooded until sleep overtook her. Then, as if some self-destructive demon was urging her on, she began to visit the open spaces where street artists performed for the public. She expected to be further crushed, finally rid of her foolish ambition to be an artist of repute. But what she found was not what she anticipated.

The street artists performed wherever crowds might gather, and they were vigorous in soliciting payment from their audiences. Often children accompanied them to prod the watchers with collecting boxes while the display was in progress, and there were few who refused to surrender a coin or two. The artists' creations were quite unlike those she had seen in the exhibition halls: they conjured dancing harlequins in gaudy costumes, blossoming flowers of the most exotic nature, exploding fireworks which filled the air with a profusion of vibrant colours. Here the emphasis was very much on movement and small-scale vitality, on brilliant, fleeting effects. Without exception, all the creations were deliberately fashioned with an excess of ambition so that they dissolved away within minutes of their emergence, leaving nothing but dust behind.

Ophre's display was something new again, his creations seemingly designed to provoke his audiences as much as entertain them. Shubi did not know what to make of it all.

Ophre listened in silence while she jabbered out her story.

24

He hurried her along winding streets, occasionally glancing back over his shoulder. Shubi was certain he was checking that the soldiers weren't following them.

At length he paused on the corner of a small square. He gripped both her wrists and peered hard into her face.

'Let me tell you something,' he said with a soft vehemence. 'Those displays you saw at the gallery, they were nothing. *Nothing*. Official art, that's all, grandiose glorifications of slaughter. The artists who created them were donkeys, nodding their heads to their masters' orders. They're celebrated because they're approved, *not* because they're good. Their work is obscene, it achieves nothing but a fawning grandiloquence. We're opposed to everything they stand for.'

She had never before heard art discussed with such passion.

'We?' she said.

Without answering, he yanked her across the square towards an open-fronted building with a gilded lantern hanging above it. No one was sitting at the tables outside, but there was plenty of activity beyond the beaded curtain.

Before they went in, Ophre told her that he and like-minded artists were interested in art for everyone, in works which illuminated, however fleetingly, the grey lives of the ordinary folk who laboured under the oppressive rule of the Hierarch Andrak and all his servants. By satirizing public figures, they hoped to highlight injustices with the aim of stirring the hearts and minds of the common people. They wanted to help them recover their dignity, courage and their yearning for justice so that ultimately they might rise up and overthrow those who oppressed them. Their art was a means to an end rather than an end in itself.

Ophre pushed aside the curtain and drew her inside. The place was filled with heat and arguments, packed with a host of jabbering, gesticulating figures. Shubi immediately knew she had found a home.

Hell's bones, it was cold! Shubi couldn't feel her feet, and her hands were turning white over the nub of her stick.

'Here, old woman.'

A young man, poorly dressed and unshaven, was thrusting a jug of spiced wine at her. She took it from him, leaning back

25

against the wall and wrapping both hands around it. Her stick clattered on the cobbles, but a woman retrieved it for her. Possibly she was the man's wife, or perhaps his sister. Both had a similar stamp of poverty on them.

'He's late,' the man remarked. 'What if he doesn't come?'

'He'll be here,' Shubi assured him.

She gulped at the wine, feeling it burn through her. It sloshed around in the bottom of the jug as she thrust it back at the man.

'Finish it off,' he said. 'You look as if you need it.'

He would come, she was sure of that. This was his first major exhibition, the breakthrough long anticipated and now finally at hand. Everything lay before him now; nothing could stand in his way provided he kept his head.

She'd had her own moment of glory once, many years ago. For him it would be more lasting, she was sure. His gift was so exceptional only madness or death could deny it.

'Shubi! Shubi!'

Ophre and the others were beckoning her out on to the stage. She shook her head, retreating into the wings, clutching her cloak around herself.

Ophre strode after her. 'What's the matter?'

'I can't do it.'

'Of course you can.'

She shook her head again.

He gripped her arms. 'It's easy. Once you get out there, the fear goes away.'

She wished she could believe the assurance in his voice.

'I'll never be able to concentrate.'

'It's only people. Ordinary people like us.'

She peered out at the crowd assembled in the park. A thin autumn rain was falling, but the people had turned out in force, most of them commoners, the city's poor. So far the demonstration had been a great success, with Ophre and other artists conjuring a series of prancing stereotypes of the military and nobility, much to the delight of everyone.

'There isn't a soldier in sight,' Ophre remarked.

'I know. I'm not afraid of them.'

The fact that they had been allowed to construct a crude

26

stage overnight without hindrance seemed to indicate a lack of leadership in the Hierarchy. Andrak had died only two days ago, and his son and successor, Jormalu, was a young man who had been pampered by his father. The movement to which the artists at the Golden Lamp were attached had decided on a mass demonstration and celebration in Temple Park, the city's largest, and word of mouth had brought people from all over Veridi-Almar to watch the scabrous entertainments and listen to inflammatory speeches.

'You can't turn back now,' Ophre insisted. 'You'll always regret it.'

Still she hesitated. She had already told him of the creation she planned to fashion for the event. Since her association with him her creations had acquired a new complexity, become less idealized and more reflective of people's lives. She could not possibly let him down now.

Pushing past him, she limped out on to the stage. It was rickety and slick with moisture, and she prayed she wouldn't fall.

The inspiration for her creation had come from a fortuitous incident. Several days before, after a morning spent putting creases into fine gowns and tunics, she went walking and found herself in the big square opposite the High Temple. There were soldiers everywhere, holding back a curious crowd.

Presently a robed priestess emerged from the temple, accompanied by a squat man swathed in plum and cream silks. It was none other than Andrak's son and successor. Jormalu had reached full manhood, but his smooth face retained the plumpness of childhood indulgence. His father was lying in state inside the temple, and he had evidently been paying his respects. After bidding farewell to the priestess, he motioned to a soldier, who led forward a huge black horse.

The horse was far larger than any of his cavalrymen, and Jormalu needed the assistance of two soldiers to haul himself up into the saddle. As he rode off in all dignity across the square, he looked absurd.

Shubi studied her audience as the spirits gathered around her. There were people perched in trees, people clustered on the autumn green grass, on the roofs and balconies of the houses bordering the park. All were heedless of the rain, and all were waiting.

27

Her head filled with a gush of spirits as she closed her eyes and concentrated on the image of the enormous black horse with the tiny Jormalu on its back. She added a few flourishes, emblazoning the words THE PEOPLE across the buttocks of the beast and making Jormalu grossly fat and spindly limbed, his face consumed with terror.

She felt an overwhelming surge of release, and opened her eyes to see her creation blink into existence centre-stage. It was full of colour and detail and life. She could almost smell the sweat on the horse's flanks, see the veins in its eyeballs, hear the whimper in Jormalu's knotted throat. It was exactly as she had imagined it.

The horse reared and bucked, throwing the hapless young Hierarch right off the stage into the mud in front of it. The crowd erupted with approval.

Both horse and Hierarch dissolved away a few moments later, but still the cheering went on. Staring into the wings, Shubi saw Ophre and several other artists grinning and applauding. For the first time in her life, she felt completely fulfilled.

Then she heard a noise above the cheers – a rumbling, thunderous sound. The crowd surged, and people began shouting with alarm as horsebacked soldiers burst from every street and alleyway around the park.

Preceded by a great clattering, the carriage turned into the avenue.

The crowd immediately drew itself up. Pulled by two piebald horses, the carriage was black with gold trim, heavy embroidered drapes hanging at the windows.

It ground to a halt outside the house, steam rising from the horses' flanks. Two coachmen jumped down from the front and began marshalling the crowd until there was a corridor to the house's entranceway. Then the carriage's doors were opened.

The Lady Orizay was the first to emerge. She was an elegant and icily attractive woman of middle years, dressed in deep red silks, her fiery hair cropped short. Lord Orizay followed, a suave and handsome man with a sallow complexion and hair that gleamed with oil. He wore a flounced black tunic.

And finally the artist himself. Shubi found herself retreating, making sure that others were hiding her from sight. Here he was, a preposterous pink cloak draped over his shoulders, modelled in style after the dark blue one she had worn for years. He was as handsome as ever, fully the young man now, approaching the peak of his physical prime, at the beginning of a glorious career. And he had lost none of his charm, nodding and smiling, taking people's hands to kiss as Lord and Lady Orizay led him forward, up the steps.

Lord Orizay paused in the open doorway to address the crowd.

'We shall need a few minutes to ensure that everything is in order inside. I trust we can rely on your indulgence. You will all be admitted as soon as possible.'

Then the house swallowed up all three, the door closing heavily behind them.

'Shubi!'

She could still hear his prim nasal voice calling up the stairs as she was busy changing the sheets on his bed. A pomegranate. The damned fool had sent her out for a pomegranate.

Shubi haggled absentmindedly with the stallholder, a plump fruit already in her hand. Around her the market-place seethed with people, the air heavy with the smell of trodden peaches and mangoes. The evening was hot and airless, and she quickly tired of bargaining. Surrendering some coins, she retrieved her stick and pushed off through the crowd.

The stick was useful for prodding people who stood in her way, though it was scarcely consolation for the perpetual ache in her hip. She slipped the pomegranate into the pocket of her cloak, aware that she had paid twice the price Begalket had ordered. He was such a miser, that man, a miser and a prig. She had been his housekeeper ever since her return to Veridi-Almar, and she had developed a thorough dislike of him and all his spoiled pupils.

A horse-drawn cart laden with grapes trundled by, only narrowly missing her. She crossed the street and began climbing an alleyway, her breath rattling in her throat. It wasn't the quickest way back, but she needed to get out of the heat and the noise. Since her exile, she found too great a press of people unbearable.

A pomegranate. That petulant brat Erice had insisted she

29

wanted one, and of course Begalket was instantly ready to oblige her. No doubt the fact that her father was a minor official in the Hierarchy made him more than usually eager to please her.

She turned a corner, found the sun in her face, headed up another narrow street. Presently she came upon a small square which she recognized immediately.

Directly opposite her on the corner was a large booth selling lottery tickets. The ornate lantern and the outside tables were gone, but there was no mistaking what had once been the Golden Lamp.

She continued on without pause, stick knocking on the hard-packed earth. The survivors of those days were in hiding, and they were few. Of Ophre and his closest friends, nothing was known. Most likely they had been murdered and their bodies disposed of.

When the soldiers invaded the park she had been knocked down by a horse and woke crammed into the back of a wagon with a dozen other women. They were part of a convoy, heading south. Many days later they arrived in the rainforest where Jormalu was having a winter palace built, a grand project which would take years to complete. There they were put to work serving food for the male prisoners who hauled the stones from nearby quarries. They lived in insanitary tents and the days and months blended into a meaningless haze of illness and exhaustion. Her hip worsened in the humid climate until she could walk only with the aid of a stick, and hope of release dwindled until she lost track of how long she had been in exile.

Then, one morning, she and the other women were bundled into wagons once more. Shubi was certain they were being taken to a place of execution; but instead they began the long journey back to Veridi-Almar. Jormalu had declared an amnesty for all criminals to celebrate the birth of his first son. The wagons took them to the outskirts of the city, and they were set free.

Five years had passed. Her old room was occupied, but for once luck was with her: the caretaker let her sleep in a storeroom and share his food. He knew of a man, he said, a tutor to the children of the rich, who was seeking a woman to tend his house. He would recommend her if she wished.

Shubi seized the opportunity. Begalket condescended to take

her on as his housekeeper after only the briefest of interviews. She soon discovered why. He was scrupulous to the point of fanaticism about neatness and cleanliness, forever running his fingers over furniture and peering under chairs to ensure she had left no trace of dust. He paid her a pittance, yet expected her to work from dawn to midnight. But Shubi found advantages in her situation. Begalket gave her a small attic room where she lived rent free, and she performed her duties stoically while he sat in his study with a succession of children from well-heeled families who had been sent to him to have their minds improved. For Shubi, the quietness of the house and the mindless nature of her duties were a blessing; having lost all ambition, she was blissfully free of expectation. What she craved most was a life of peaceful solitude.

Yet she was not entirely alone. During the rigours of her exile, she had had no strength or inclination to practise her art and grew oblivious of the spirits. Since her return, they had begun to make their presence felt. But she was obdurate in refusing to entertain them; they were a part of her life which she now considered closed.

Where the devil was she? She looked up and down the unfamiliar street, certain she should have known it but not recognizing anything. She climbed a short flight of steps, paused to watch three children chasing one another around an old stone pillory. Then onwards, stick tapping, chest rattling.

Here the tall overhanging buildings blocked out the sun. Rubbish was strewn everywhere, and the stink from the gutters was overwhelming.

A breeze seemed to spring up, and she shuddered, stopping in her tracks.

Another cluster of children were sitting on a flight of steps outside one building. All were young, grubby, dressed in ragged clothes. One of them, a boy of about ten with hair as blond as wheat, was entertaining the others with a display of brightly coloured scarves which whirled and swooped in the air above his head.

Shubi shuffled forward, still staring. There was no wind in the street, but the soughing in her ears grew stronger. The scarves were silken, their colours brilliantly rich crimsons, purples, deep

31

greens and golds. They spun and flapped, spiralled around one another, then burst effortlessly apart.

The boy was a beautiful bronzed child despite the green pearl which drooled from one nostril and the griminess of his rough linen shirt. His teeth gleamed as he smiled, enjoying the attentions of his friends. At the same time he was hardly concerned with what he had created, not looking up once as the scarves continued their hectic dance. Chimeras swirled and raged invisibly around him. In all her years she had never seen such intensely vivid and energetic art-forms.

The children became aware of her, and the boy leapt up, thrusting out his hand.

'Did you do that?' Shubi asked, knowing full well he had.

He nodded, palm pleading for a coin.

'What's your name?' Shubi asked, finding it hard to keep the excitement from her voice.

'Neni. I want money for supper.'

Shubi reached out and seized his wrist, now possessed with the certainty that her life had taken yet another turn.

'Money?' she said, and cackled. 'Money?' She pulled a handkerchief from her cloak pocket and swabbed his nose. 'You want money?' He wriggled in her grip, trying to break free. She held him firm, held him hard. 'I'm going to give you much more than money, boy!'

She moved slowly around the hall, studying the exhibits, always keeping a crowd between herself and the recess where the artist was receiving the congratulations of his audience. The sun was now shining in through the windows, flooding the place with light.

He had not failed her, not in the least, even though the exhibition was like nothing she had anticipated. Its theme was a simple one – *Love* – and he had produced a series of life-sized nudes and family portraits of parents and children. Some of the poses were erotic, but none were obscene. In one, he had even introduced a note of macabre whimsy, depicting a man about to behead with an axe a woman wrapped against the body of her lover on a turbulent sea of white sheets.

Religious convention did not permit completely mobile human figures, but many of the exhibits had been given gentle movement, often to sensuous effect. All were remarkably life-like. She knew no other artist who could fashion the human form so accurately, with such realism: some of the figures could hardly be distinguished from the people who were gazing at them.

When she thought no one was looking, she touched the flank of a child holding the disembodied arm of its father. The flesh was cold, but it yielded to her touch just like real flesh. He had given all the creations full solidity, and they were so well formed they would probably keep their colour and movement for months or even years. And when they finally turned to stone, it would be hard and durable, like granite or marble. They would become statues, attaining a different kind of lasting beauty.

She glanced at him again and saw him sharing a few private words with Lady Orizay, their faces close to one another. He called himself Vendavo now, a grander, more imposing name, though to her he would always be Neni. *Love*. It was not the theme she had expected of him, not at all. It made his creations even more remarkable that they sprang from a mind which she was not sure had ever experienced the real meaning of the word.

'Shubi . . . Shubi . . .'

He was whispering into her face, his breath rank. She closed her eyes, doing her best to breathe in without wheezing as he flailed away at her on the creaking bed. She couldn't remember his name, and was surprised he was using hers. Most called out other names, the names of wives and lovers, of those they despised yet had to possess.

The way he was going at it, it would soon be over, praise fortune. Better get him out before Neni returned from his lessons, otherwise the boy would start asking awkward questions. Of course he probably knew full well how she supported the two of them; he had an old head on his shoulders and was a charmer with women himself. But she didn't want him walking in to see her legs still spread wide.

A strenuous grunt, and then he slumped, crushing her with his stale-sweat body. Hell's bones, most of them didn't even bother to wash! She could feel him shrivelling inside her while his heart throbbed triumphantly against her breast. She moved, and he slipped out of her. Then he rolled away.

She sat up, reaching for her skirt.

'How much?' he asked.

She repeated the amount they had negotiated at the start. He rummaged in his shirt, his back to her, and finally put a few notes down on the bed. He dressed quickly and departed without another word.

Six grubby notes lay on the bed; he'd left her a tip! She rolled them up and wedged them into the gap above the door lintel. Then she boiled water and washed herself thoroughly.

An unguarded glimpse of her reflection in the mirror startled her, as if she was seeing her face for the first time in years. With her sagging skin and greying hair she was turning into a scarecrow. Little wonder that most of her customers were equally wretched; her limp and wheeze didn't help.

She tidied the bed, then opened the blind to let in the air. Below in the courtyard three boys were tormenting a ginger cat. She yelled at them, and they scampered away down the alley. They looked as waif-like as Neni the first time she'd encountered him. Five years on, he was becoming quite a cultured young man, though the shrewdness of the streets would never leave him.

Half the money she earned went on Begalket's fees, but it gave her great satisfaction to be his paymaster rather than him hers. And of course the boy was receiving a steady education into the bargain; as much as she loathed Begalket, she knew he was a good teacher, and the boy would learn discipline from his fussiness into the bargain. Without her, he'd probably still be on the streets, doing brilliant but fleeting creations for unappreciative passersby. Or he might have ended up with a blade through his temple and his gifts extinguished for ever.

She put a pot of rice on the hotplate, added barley and the scraps of mutton she'd scavenged from one of the stalls at the market. Neni could have those; meat tended to make her bilious these days.

She'd been determined to have the boy for her own. He wouldn't tell her where he lived, but the other children – his brothers and sisters it turned out – took her upstairs. She met the father, a slovenly man in a grimy vest who looked like a child-beater, and the mother, morose and apathetic. They cared nothing for their son's talents, and so Shubi made her offer there and then. She would take the boy and raise him herself.

The parents debated only briefly, and it was clear to her that they considered the boy just another mouth to feed. Finally the father said that they would agree to hand the boy over to her, if they were compensated. She offered them half her savings, money wrung like blood from Begalket's stony heart. They began to haggle, and finally settled for half as much again.

The boy said nothing throughout. She took him aside and asked if he was aware of the strength of his gift. He shrugged. So she proceeded to tell him how his life might be transformed if he allowed his abilities to be developed under the guidance of someone who could also fashion chimeras, someone like herself. She could turn his raw talent into a finely tuned art, bring him wealth and fame, make him the envy of everyone in the city.

No doubt she oversold her case, for she knew better than anyone that there were no certainties in her profession. But the potential was undoubtedly there. And the boy's blue eyes widened as she painted his glorious future. She could tell that he already possessed a strong streak of independence and self-assurance, and he did not even bother to glance at his parents before saying that he would go with her.

She gave Begalket her notice that very day, and used what remained of her savings to rent rooms where she and the boy could live. And then his education began in earnest. Shubi was determined to improve his mind as well as his creative gifts, and she offered to spend her mornings cleaning Begalket's house if he would in exchange give the boy free lessons. Begalket, hard to please though he was, knew that she had given him good service, and grudgingly agreed to the proposition.

But now she was left with the problem of finding money for them to live. So, when the boy was at his afternoon tutorials, she took men into her bed. She had never been a beauty and was physically well past her prime, but there were always those who wanted the services she was prepared to render. She could not have earned as much money in any other way.

In the evenings, she practised with the boy, teaching him all the fundamentals of concentration, patience, imagination and control. He had an exceptionally vivid mind, but it was quite undisciplined. She would set him exercises, asking him to fashion something which she knew might give him difficulty. He liked to think boldly, in strong colours, with lots of movement, so she encouraged him to produce still-lifes, objects in pastel shades, to replicate unhurried movements like the billowing of clouds, someone stirring from sleep, a caterpillar moving along a leaf-stalk, smoke from a fire rising on a still day. He tended to visualize in a broad dramatic way and was sometimes neglectful of subtle detail. She took him to the High Temple and made him stare at it for an entire morning, studying every corner and crevice, every facet of its rich ornamentation, before taking him home and demanding he reproduce it in miniature. She made him do it several times until she was satisfied with the result.

He hated the exercises, the strictures she was constantly imposing on him. And at first he was easily daunted, flying into a temper or descending into sullenness if he failed to achieve what she wanted. But at the same time she could sense his growing ambition, his desire to perfect his art, his determination to measure up to whatever standards she set. For Shubi it was the most exciting time of her life.

Eventually she began taking him into parks and squares to perform for others. There he produced some remarkable creations – complex crystalline shapes which spun and cartwheeled overhead, intensely localized storms and blizzards which made the crowds reel back in alarm, characters and creatures, scenes and situations more vivid and lifelike than any she had ever seen before. All his creations were designed for a brief brilliance before they faded into dust; she trained him to do it that way, knowing that the authorities disliked street artists cluttering up the parks and public places with stony residues of their displays. The crowds looked on in silent wonder, some admiring, many perplexed. Few offered coins, and most drifted away with a disgruntled air. Shubi became convinced that they considered the boy too young for his gifts. They were not prepared to shower their adulation on a child unless someone gave them a precedent. And no precedent was forthcoming.

But Shubi persevered, comforting and cajoling the boy whenever he became downcast. Sooner or later you'll be recognized, she would tell him; sooner or later your time will come. He had the resilience of youth, and there were other compensations. He remained a very handsome boy, and women of all ages were

36

easily beguiled by his brilliant smile, his azure eyes, the eyes of an angel. Often he came home late from Begalket's, usually, Shubi suspected, because of liaisons with girls whose hearts he doubtless broke quite effortlessly. She couldn't really begrudge him such dalliances, because she worked him hard at all other times. He also kept in contact with his brothers and sisters, but never to her knowledge visited his parents again.

She battled on against all frustrations, but still no one would recognize the boy's talents. Then the Hierarchy enacted a series of reforms, one of which involved the opening of small galleries where street artists could show their work, providing that it had no 'dangerous' content. Well, the boy was not politically minded at all, and she increased her quota of men until she had sufficient money to rent a gallery near the waterfront where a selection of the boy's latest creations was displayed for several days.

There were a respectable number of visitors, some of them wealthy folk whom Shubi did her best to persuade to become the boy's patrons. But while most were genuinely admiring of his prowess, none were actually prepared to use their money and influence to promote his career. Like the crowds in the park, they lacked the courage of their instincts.

Still, the exhibition had not been a total loss. It had broadened the audience for the boy's work, and Shubi was already saving hard for another. In the end, someone would 'discover' him, she was convinced. A talent like his could not be denied for ever.

The rice was cooked, and she took the pot off the hotplate. Outside, dusk was encroaching, and she lit an oil-lamp, her shadow looming on the wall. She sat down to wait. And to wait. She'd bought an old doorless wardrobe where she kept a selection of his work, still-lifes and miniatures. Figures and scenes so finely wrought she sometimes found it hard to believe that the boy had created them, even though she'd been there at the time. His larger, more mobile works were given away to friends and acquaintances or simply vanished of their own accord, some drifting out through the window to disappear over the rooftops. Shubi would sometimes imagine them floating down quiet streets, hovering in squares, drawing astonished gazes from people who knew nothing of their creator. The boy seldom showed much interest in them once they were finished;

the act of creation was far more important to him than the end product.

It had been a hard day, Begalket at his most demanding, a succession of customers manhandling her all afternoon. She turned the oil-lamp up against the darkness. Sooner or later the boy would come. She closed her eyes, dozed.

A creaking on the stairs awoke her, and she immediately recognized Neni's tread. Relief swept her weariness away. The door opened and he walked in.

He was a young man now, childhood almost entirely gone from his face. He wore a clean sand-coloured tunic and strong leather boots; she always made sure he was properly dressed. But there was something uncharacteristically hesitant in his manner. He lingered on the threshold, the door still open.

'You're late,' she remarked.

'I had to see someone.'

He wasn't looking at her. She reached for her stick, said, 'Oh?'

A woman entered. She was about five years older than Neni, blonde like him, attractive in a rather brittle way. An expensive embroidered gown swathed her slender body. Her face seemed familiar, but Shubi couldn't place her.

'This is Leraine,' Neni said. 'Remember her?'

Shubi leant on her stick, still sitting. The name meant nothing.

'We met at the exhibition,' the woman said, her tone polite but formal.

Shubi remembered. She had come to the exhibition and had lingered for some hours, admiring Neni's work and also spending time in conversation with him. Her father had some sort of minor position in the Hierarchy, she couldn't recall what. The family would be moderately well-off and comfortable, but not so influential that Shubi had thought it worthwhile propositioning her for a patronage.

A look passed between Neni and Leraine, and Shubi immediately understood that the two of them were lovers. They had probably been so since the exhibition. But there was more.

'Neni is extremely talented,' Leraine remarked.

'Indeed,' Shubi agreed. 'It's a shame we haven't yet convinced more people of that fact.'

'Perhaps he needs better connections.'

Shubi rose from her chair, taking her time over it. Neni was looking at her now, but there was a blankness in his eyes, a shutting down and cutting off.

'You may well be right,' Shubi said to Leraine. 'Do you have something to propose?'

'We love each other,' Leraine said bluntly.

Shubi was still looking at Neni, and she was sure of another thing: he would not have used the word 'love' to describe whatever there was between them. But he held his peace, showing a sudden interest in one of the figures on his wardrobe shelf.

'He's met my parents,' Leraine went on, 'and they all admire one another. Father agrees with me about his gifts and feels that his work should be better known.'

Shubi could imagine the boy charming them with his glittering smile and dazzling eyes.

'Is your father proposing to become his patron?' she asked.

'Were we wealthy he'd have no hesitation,' Leraine replied, 'but unfortunately that isn't possible. However he is prepared to provide him with rooms where he can live and work.'

'Ah,' said Shubi. 'So you're proposing he move in with you.'

'We're all agreed that it would be for the best.'

Shubi turned to Neni. 'Are *you* agreed?'

He replaced the figurine he had been holding.

'Leraine and I want to be together, and we have her parents' blessing.' He gave her his best smile. 'I can't thank you enough for everything you've done for me. I know it's been hard, and I can't expect you to keep giving up everything for my sake. This way it will be easier for all of us.'

Effortless words, sugared by his smile. Shubi wanted to laugh at the suggestion that he was doing it for her. She wanted to scream at him, to say that he owed her everything. He hadn't even had the courage to tell her himself but had let the woman do it for him.

She said nothing, offered not the slightest hint of an objection. A part of her had always known that something like this might happen. It had come more abruptly, more shockingly, than she had anticipated, but she was too weary for the fight. Let him go, she thought, steadying herself on her stick; you could never keep him anyway. The rice would be cold by now. Let him go.

39

'Then,' she said softly, 'you have my blessing.'

He came forward and embraced her, murmuring his thanks, his promise to visit her regularly. Meanwhile Leraine looked on with relief and triumph.

Lord Orizay clapped his hands, bade the crowd pay attention.

'Vendavo would like to say a few words to you before we leave.'

The crowd, respectfully subdued in any case, became positively hushed. The artist rose to address them.

'I don't have much to say,' he began. 'I deal in visions, not words. But I'd like to thank every one of you for coming today. You are the people who've made this exhibition a success. I'd also like to express my deepest gratitude towards Lord and Lady Orizay for sponsoring me and allowing me the use of their beautiful house for the display. Without their support, none of this would have been possible.'

A glance back at the two, smiles between all three. Lord Orizay held a senior position in the Hierarchy, and his wife had long been a collector of chimera-art. She was also reputed to have a powerful appetite for young lovers. It had taken Neni less than a year to make himself known to them through the intermediary of Leraine's father; soon they were actively promoting his career. He was still not formally recognized as an official artist – his work was too brilliant and unpredictable for that – but apparently Jormalu did not look unfavourably on it and put no obstacles in the way of the exhibition.

Rumour had also reached Shubi that Leraine had tried to kill herself after Neni deserted her for Lord Orizay's household. Her father had later married her off to a wine-merchant, and she was now carrying their second child. Life was simply unstoppable.

'There's one other person I'd like to thank,' the artist was continuing. 'A woman none of you will have ever heard of. She took me off the streets when I was young and cared for me. She was an artist herself, and she taught me how to harness my gifts. Without her care and guidance, I would never have achieved anything worthwhile.'

Shubi was convinced he knew she was in the hall. He was going to name her, point her out to the crowd. She tried to shrink in on herself, to hide from sight.

'She's dead now. A fever took her, and she passed away in my arms some years ago. I'd like to dedicate this exhibition to her memory.'

Applause rang in her ears. She felt herself teetering on her stick, but clung on with every shred of her strength. She still had all his old works in her room. They would be valuable now, but she'd never sell any.

The crowd began to retreat as Neni, flanked by Lord and Lady Orizay, was shepherded towards the exit. Shubi suddenly realized she was directly in their path. She tried to move back, but the crowd wouldn't let her. Her stick wobbled, then slid away as she went crashing to her hands and knees, right in front of him.

He halted, but three retainers swept in front of him and hauled her to her feet. The crowd had their arms outstretched and he began grasping their hands, his attention already diverted as she was bundled to a chair. She caught a final glimpse of his hair, like a flash of sunlight, as he swept through the exit to the waiting coach.

2

Birth-Rites

1

'There it is,' Vendavo told her, peering out of the carriage window.

Only now did Nyssa draw the curtains back. It was the first time she had ridden in a horse-drawn coach – she just an orphan from the poor quarter of Veridi-Almar – and she couldn't face the curious glances from passersby when they had set off from their house in the city. Vendavo, by contrast, had enjoyed the journey, waving to people in the street. Many had recognized him. His fame still seemed rather strange to her, for she knew little about his art. That he had married her in the first place was another wonder; but then, she had never imagined she would be carrying her first child at sixteen.

Heshezz's residence sat in the middle of a scrubby plain north-east of Veridi-Almar. White walls enclosed it, and behind them stood a screen of closely planted cypresses. Nearby was a long low building with horses and several soldiers outside. It was a barracks, Nyssa realized, no doubt for Heshezz's household guard.

They approached the house down a dusty road which led to intricate wrought-iron gates flanked by more soldiers. The carriage rocked gently, adding to Nyssa's discomfort. It seemed an age since they had set off from the city, and the baby was pressing on her bladder. She felt as if it was straining to burst out of her, eager to begin its life. It would be a joy to climb a flight of stairs again without having to pause for breath.

She heard voices, the gates creaking open, then they moved on. She felt nervous, still wondering why Heshezz had sent for her husband.

Vendavo, leaning out the window, said, 'Look, Nyssa!'

She peered through her own window. The spacious grounds of the house were carefully cultivated with a variety of exotic bushes and flowers. Everywhere the grass was richer and greener than any she had ever seen. It was hard to believe that the city and its outlying provinces had been in the grip of a drought since spring.

But her husband wasn't simply referring to the vegetation, she quickly saw. Several kinds of long-tailed pheasant strolled through clearings, and in the trees she glimpsed bright-plumaged birds. The air was thick with the perfumes of flowers, dense with clouds of flies.

She shifted laboriously on her seat. Her bottom had gone numb, her back was aching, and she longed to be let out of the carriage. Finally the horses drew up outside the main entrance.

The house looked almost modest in comparison with its grounds. It was a square white two-storeyed building with a red-tiled roof and a large arched entranceway. A group of white-suited servants were waiting outside. Tender hands took her, helping her up the steps. Vendavo was already striding ahead into a spacious marble hall.

Nyssa splashed water on her face and neck, then dabbed herself dry, relishing the fragrance of the towel which had been provided for her.

When she emerged, she found her husband sitting alone in the reception room, a pitcher of red grape juice on the low table in front of him.

'Have you seen him yet?' she asked.

'Not yet. We'll be dining with him shortly.'

She sat down beside him. 'Has anyone said why you were sent for?'

Vendavo shook his head, a distant expression on his face. He was staring at one of the richly patterned carpets which hung on the walls, its design a mass of curlicues and lozenges in golds and browns. He did not seem the slightest bit anxious, was not at all in awe of Heshezz's reputation.

It was blissfully cool in the room. Nyssa kicked off her shoes and draped her ankles across a padded footstool. Still she could not rid herself of her nervousness. Vendavo had insisted she accompany him despite the advanced stage of her pregnancy. In many ways he was still a mystery to her. She had been as surprised as anyone when he had asked her to marry him after declaring before a witness that the child she was carrying was his. Lord and Lady Orizay had been arrested just days later, and she often wondered whether Vendavo was forewarned and married her to make himself respectable. Nyssa knew she was pretty, but she had never pretended she was clever or understood anything about Vendavo's art. The Lady Orizay had plucked her out of the kitchens because of her looks, and she, being a practically minded girl, had no qualms about sharing her bed because it meant better food, fine dresses and a room of her own. It was in bed with the Lady that she had first met her husband.

Of course the Lady Orizay had brought disaster on her own head by seducing a nephew of Jormalu's who could not resist boasting of his exploits publicly. Jormalu, like his father before him, was prepared to tolerate any indiscretion as long as it did not become a matter of common gossip. So he had exiled his nephew to a bleak northern province and had the Lord and Lady Orizay executed for 'corrupting public morals'.

Nyssa poured herself a cup of grape juice and drank it down. She and Vendavo had been lucky to survive the scandal, for they were both favourites of the Lady. Perhaps Vendavo's popularity had protected them. He often performed in public places and was adored by the commonfolk. And he had moved swiftly to arrange a very public wedding once she had agreed to marriage. She was not certain the child was his, though she had never told him as much. Though the wedding was a success, Vendavo had remained under something of a cloud. He continued working in the modest house they bought on the Almar bank of the river, but there were no exhibitions of his chimeras, no more performances for the people. Heshezz's summons was the first official acknowledgement of his existence since the scandal.

Vendavo had closed his eyes. Nyssa strained forward to put her cup down on the table. A fat black insect with golden wings shimmered into existence above Vendavo's head. It hovered for a second, then spiralled towards the balcony window, disappearing into the garden over a tangle of honeysuckle.

At that moment a servant entered and announced that Heshezz was ready to receive them.

Heshezz stood at the end of a long table. He was a tall, lean man of advancing years, his head entirely shaven, his hooked nose and hooded eyes giving him a sinister aspect. He wore a blue and gold ceremonial uniform, one breast covered with the decorations bestowed on him during his long command of both Andrak and Jormalu's fleets. He motioned them to chairs on either side of him.

A door opened at the other end of the room, and a plump man in crumpled brown robes entered with a young woman. She was slim and handsome, her jet-black hair emphasized by the pallor of her skin and the white gown which she wore.

'This is my daughter, Rianth,' Heshezz said. 'She's convalescing after an illness.' He indicated the man. 'And this is Khendra, her physician. There is no need to stand up.'

Nyssa had been about to rise. She froze like a timid pup called to heel. Heshezz introduced her husband as 'Vendavo, the renowned artist', and herself as 'his wife, who you can see is full of his child'.

Khendra seated Rianth next to Vendavo before taking a chair beside Nyssa. A trio of servants entered with food and wine.

The meal was a stiff affair, the conversation halting and strained. Heshezz indicated his impatience with small-talk by the curtness of his replies, and Vendavo fell to asking Rianth about the birds in the garden. During his many voyages, Heshezz had collected specimens of birds and plants from distant lands, and Rianth joked that this was her father's only passion apart from making enemies.

Nyssa had no appetite, and she saw that Rianth also ate little. She felt in awe of Heshezz, even though he paid her no attention. His reputation was that of a severe and uncompromising commander. He more than anyone had been responsible for maintaining the Hierarchy's self-imposed isolation, his fleets patrolling the surrounding oceans and turning away vessels from other lands. Nyssa wondered if the treasures of his garden had been forcibly taken from foreign merchantmen. She felt like a child in his presence who might be summarily dismissed from the table for the slightest breach of etiquette. But then Khendra began jabbering to her in between swallowing mouthfuls of wine. When was her child due? Was it her first? Had she had a comfortable pregnancy? She stammered out answers as best she could. Khendra wiped his hands on a napkin before putting them lingeringly on her waist. Finally he announced that she had good hips for child-bearing.

A selection of fruits was offered by the servants. Both Nyssa and Rianth declined.

'In that case,' Heshezz said to his daughter, 'you may leave us.'

It was plain to Nyssa that she was also included in the dismissal. She followed Rianth into another room whose balcony windows were wide open. Rianth suggested they sit outside. A variety of cushions had been placed in the shade, and Nyssa managed to settle herself amongst them. A climbing plant with violet bell-shaped flowers covered the balcony rail, its spicy perfume filling the air.

'Have you and Vendavo been married long?' Rianth asked.

'No,' said Nyssa. 'Not long.'

'I hope to have children some day. Ordeshe wants many sons. He's my suitor, a young officer. But first I have to recover my health.'

She lay with her head back and her eyes closed. She had talked quite animatedly to Vendavo during the meal but now looked exhausted.

'My mother died giving birth to me,' she remarked. 'My father never remarried. I always used to wish I had brothers and sisters.'

'What illness have you had?' Nyssa asked gently.

'Khendra says it's a disorder of the digestive system. He thinks it may have been brought on by eating spoiled fruit.'

'But you're better now?'

'Oh, yes. On the road to recovery, Khendra says.'

But her voice sounded weak and tired. Nyssa felt her own discomforts were trivial in comparison. She judged that Rianth was perhaps a year or two older than herself.

'I've seen your husband's work,' Rianth said. 'It's wonderful. Do you know why my father sent for him?'

'I – he hasn't said.'

Rianth kept her eyes closed. 'It's odd. He's never shown any interest in artists before now. He's always preferred living things, birds especially.'

So even his daughter didn't know. Nyssa felt a renewed

anxiety. But surely Heshezz wouldn't have let them dine with him if Vendavo was still disapproved of?

'Of course,' Rianth was saying, 'the artists in his day weren't as accomplished as your husband. I think he may want him to make chimeras of his birds. A lot of them die each winter.'

'Yes,' said Nyssa, seizing on this possibility. 'Vendavo would be happy to do that, I'm sure.'

Bees were droning among the bell-shaped flowers. Nyssa watched them climb inside, take their fill of nectar, then arc drunkenly away. The baby had begun to kick her under the ribs, and she found that remaining still was best. The garden shone in rich colours under a clear blue sky. Servants were patrolling shaded flowerbeds with huge watering cans.

Presently Rianth began to snore softly – so softly it sounded as if she was sighing. It was hot on the balcony, airless. The baby fell quiet, and she shifted her position among the cushions.

There was a flash of blue and a beating of wings. A red-throated bird appeared momentarily above the balcony, plucking a bee from the air with its long beak before vanishing from sight. For long moments there was silence. Then the bees began to drone again.

The smell of the violet flowers filled Nyssa's nostrils. The heat lay on her body like a blanket. She undid several buttons at the neck of her dress and breathed in slowly, deeply, as her doctor had advised. There, that was better. Would they be asked to stay overnight? She began to hope so, for she did not relish the journey back to Veridi-Almar. She had packed a bag of clothing in case.

A wedge of sunlight was lying on the lower half of her body. Heavenly host, she was frying under the heat! She tried to rise, failed utterly. The child began kicking again, battering her ribs. Rianth was sleeping so peacefully Nyssa couldn't bring herself to call out. Once more she heaved herself up, then slumped back, defeated. It had been so easy to settle herself among the cushions she had not considered how difficult it would be to rise from them. A flush of heat rose up from her legs like a wave that engulfed her.

He was smiling down at her with his perfect white teeth. No doubt about it, she had snared a handsome man. Who was that beside him? The physician, Khendra. And Rianth was standing over her, holding a damp towel to her forehead.

Nyssa realized she was no longer lying on the balcony but in a bed in a cool white room.

'You fainted,' Khendra told her before she could say anything. 'There's nothing to worry about.'

But both he and Rianth proceeded to fuss over her until Khendra prescribed a sleeping draught and both of them withdrew.

Vendavo sat down on the bed beside her. He stroked her hair.

'What did he want?' she asked.

'Heshezz?'

She nodded.

'He wants me to create something for him. A special chimera.'

She waited, knowing from his eyes that he was eager to tell her.

He stroked her cheek with his knuckles. 'Heshezz is leaving tonight for Veridi-Almar. He'll be returning in three days' time for Rianth's eighteenth birthday. By then, he expects me to have finished the creation.'

'What creation?'

'She's dying. His daughter. She doesn't know it, of course, but she has only a matter of months left.'

2

'Come, come,' said Khendra, 'drink it down.'

Reluctantly Nyssa took the cup from him and swallowed the milk as quickly as possible. It was fortified with herbs and root-extracts, and would, according to Khendra, 'cleanse her blood and strengthen her bones'. Rianth took it daily.

It tasted foul.

'Excellent. Now let's see how the child is lying.'

Nyssa was still groggy from the sleeping draught and had awoken late. Once again reluctantly, she allowed Khendra to pull back the bedsheets and raise her nightgown to her waist. Heshezz had left instructions that he monitor her condition, but he seemed to linger over the task of prodding and probing her belly.

Finally he declared himself satisfied and withdrew. Soon afterwards there was a polite tapping on the door, and a dark-skinned maid entered with fresh sheets and towels. She was the same age as Nyssa, and doubtless from a similar background. Nyssa attempted a smile, but the maid kept her eyes lowered. There was a moment's awkward silence. Then Nyssa went out on to the balcony so that the maid could work undisturbed by her presence.

Morning was well advanced, and the full heat of the day was settling over the garden. She watched a servant run a net through a pool, dragging out dead leaves. Others were busy pruning and planting. Groups of soldiers patrolled the grounds of the house constantly to deter intruders and would-be assassins. Heshezz was obsessive about keeping his enemies out of his garden, Rianth had told her.

Presently Nyssa saw two figures on a path which wound through a bamboo grove. Rianth was dressed in her white gown, Vendavo in a sun-yellow tunic. They were talking intently, and to Nyssa it was obvious that her husband was studying Rianth's every move, her every mannerism. They paused on an ornamental bridge which arched over a pool.

The artist and his subject.

Of course Rianth did not know that Vendavo was going to create a chimera of her. She had been told that the creation was to be a replica of her mother, Marael, based on herself because of their close resemblance. Rianth was eager to cooperate, delighted that her father wanted to commemorate the mother she had never known. Heshezz had ordered that the true nature of the chimera was not to be revealed to her, on pain of death. It was a threat which even Vendavo took seriously.

'Khendra says you mustn't stay in there too long,' Rianth told Nyssa as she led her towards the aviary. It was a segmented glass dome, green fronds and palm leaves pressing against its misted panes.

'I'm fine,' Nyssa insisted. 'He fusses too much.'

'Doesn't he?' Rianth agreed with a smile.

'He's a bit wayward with his hands, too, if you ask me.'

'Really? I can't say I've noticed that.'

'He's probably better behaved with you.'

'He's terrified of my father, I know that. My mother died in his care, and I don't think my father's ever forgiven him. He's never had much use for physicians. I suppose it's because he's never been ill himself.'

Rianth opened the aviary door. The humid air assailed Nyssa even before they stepped inside. Steam rose through numerous grilles in the flagstone floor, and Rianth explained that a big fire was kept burning in the basement with shallow pans of boiling water on top of it. Servants worked day and night to maintain the correct balance of heat and moisture.

Green trees and shrubs blossomed everywhere, huge pendulous palms stretching up to the top of the dome, ferns and cacti filling the spaces below. At ground level, exotic varieties of irises, orchids and other flowers provided splashes of colour. Tiny birds darted at them, poking their beaks inside while hovering with a blur of wings, their plumage iridescent emerald, turquoise and crimson.

'Hummingbirds,' Rianth said in a whisper.

The garden alone was a splendid creation, but here inside the aviary Nyssa felt as if she had entered another world entirely. Rianth took her right into the heart of the foliage, suddenly pointing to a black and gold bird which sat on a branch close by. It had a huge vermilion plume for a tail.

'It's a bird of paradise,' she told Nyssa. 'There are four here. My father paid a fortune for them.'

The bird moved sideways along the branch until it was lost in the leaves. Nyssa gazed upwards, profoundly aware of the swell of life around her. The aviary was filled with the strange calls of birds, most of them unseen. Suddenly she was seized with the idea that she too was now trapped inside it, a specimen in Heshezz's collection. The heavy air pressed down on her, making breathing difficult. She would suffocate if she stayed here!

Turning, she fled for the exit.

Once outside, in the grassy expanses of the garden, her panic evaporated as swiftly as the mist on her forehead under the afternoon sun.

Rianth appeared.

'I'm sorry,' Nyssa immediately blurted. 'It's wonderful. I just needed some air.'

Rianth, solicitous of her condition, simply nodded and led her over to a wooden bench under the shade of a willow.

They sat in silence for a while. Nyssa felt at ease in Rianth's company, a fact which surprised her.

'Do you think,' Rianth asked presently, 'that Vendavo will be able to create a chimera that's just like my mother?'

Nyssa eyed her.

'I don't know,' she said wanly. 'I don't think he's ever been asked to do such a thing before.'

'I'm supposed to be very like her, though sometimes I wonder if my father remembers her as well as he thinks he does.'

Nyssa didn't know what to say. She had tried to argue Vendavo out of the commission, for reasons she couldn't quite explain. But her husband would have none of it in any case. Heshezz had lost his wife and was now to lose the only other person he had ever loved: he deserved a memorial to his daughter. And think of the sheer challenge it presented! Until now, artists had always been forbidden from creating chimeras which might be mistaken for living human beings, so he had to seize the opportunity. Heshezz was Jormalu's uncle, and it was reasonable to presume that the commission had official sanction at the highest level.

Soldiers on horseback were assembling at the front of the house. They carried nets of various sizes. Nyssa asked about them.

'They're off hunting strays,' Rianth told her. 'Birds and animals that have escaped the garden. There's nothing out there to support them, and they die within days unless rescued.' She shook her head. 'Sometimes I feel just like one of them. It's been over two years since I've been able to go out.'

The evening sky was ultramarine, and the insects in the garden whirred and rasped. Nyssa sat on the balcony, vainly trying to knit a shawl for the baby. She couldn't get the knack of the pins. Finally she put them aside, sighing. Ordeshe had arrived earlier, and he and Rianth had gone walking in the garden, leaving Nyssa to her own devices. Wanting company she had gone down to the kitchens, but all the servants there had treated

51

her with a stifling deference which made her realize that, as the wife of a famous artist, she was no longer one of them.

She rose, putting a hand on the small of her back to ease the ache there, and went inside. Vendavo had been given a room next to hers to use as a study. It also contained a bed so that he could sleep undisturbed by her restlessness and conserve his energies for the creation of the chimera. He had spent all afternoon and evening there, doubtless meditating on the task. She knew better than to disturb him.

She woke to darkness. A still, oppressive heat filled the room, and there was a sour taste in her throat, a heaviness in her belly.

She burped, tasting jellied partridge and Khendra's milk. Earlier she had dined with Rianth and Ordeshe, an attentive young man who talked constantly of marriage to Rianth as if unaware that she was dying. But he had been told, Nyssa knew. She wanted to hug Rianth to atone for her part in the conspiracy.

The sour taste lingered; she had over-indulged in the partridge. Above the insect sounds from the garden she heard other noises – noises which filtered through the open balcony doors from the room next to hers. The unmistakable sounds of lovemaking.

She sat up slowly and went outside. A light was burning in Vendavo's room.

From the very edge of the balcony, it was just possible for Nyssa to lean forward and see into the room. She could feel the baby beginning to protest as she pressed her belly against the railings, straining for the best view.

Vendavo had left the drapes open, and the insect net did not prevent her from seeing inside; rather it gave the whole scene a gauzy translucence. Vendavo lay naked on his back in the white bed with the dark-skinned maid straddling him. His hands were clasped to her waist while she gripped his shoulders, her head lolling, her eyes closed as she moved up and down on him. Vendavo was staring not at her face but over her shoulder. And all around the bed, drifting in the air, were phantoms of Rianth.

Nyssa understood that they were preliminary visions conjured up as studies for the final work. Vendavo had given them the barest blush of colour, but they were not solid creations: Nyssa could see the walls of the room through them, an arabesqued carpet which hung near the door, a sky-blue vase of dried flowers on a side-table. There were seven or eight in all, half of them clothed in Rianth's favourite white gown, half of them naked. They were static figures, some in demure poses, others with limbs outstretched. Even as she watched, they began to flicker, to begin the slow process of dissolving away entirely.

Meanwhile the girl continued to move on her husband's belly. Nyssa was scarcely shocked, for she knew Vendavo's appetites better than most and knew how impossible prolonged celibacy was for him. Better a maid than the daughter of his patron.

She watched the phantoms drift slowly around the bed. Vendavo had barely sketched in their facial details so that it was impossible to judge whether the final likeness would be accurate or not. Her husband was as wholly concentrated on studying them as the maid was in taking her pleasure from him.

The baby lurched in her belly, and a foul wind broke in her throat. She staggered back, fell to her knees, then began emptying her supper on to the balcony floor.

It seemed to go on and on, until finally she brought up only bile. Her eyes were glazed with tears, and she did not recognize the figure who suddenly appeared on the balcony. He lifted her up. It was Vendavo. 'There, there,' he began saying as he carried her inside and laid her on the bed. The maid was hovering in the door, a pale shift hastily thrown on.

'Fetch Khendra,' Vendavo told her sharply.

3

Nyssa and Rianth stood before a big mirror in Rianth's bed-room. They were trying on gowns. Heshezz was giving a ball to celebrate Rianth's birthday, and over a hundred guests were invited. Rianth had found Nyssa a loose pleated dress in smoky pink satin which would fit her tolerably well. She herself had chosen a cream silk gown with padded shoulders and a flounced skirt which made her look less thin; a high collar drew attention to the chiselled beauty of her face – the high cheekbones, strong nose, long neck. Her eyes were violet-blue, and for once they seemed to sparkle.

'I wish I had your freckles,' she remarked to Nyssa.

'Do you?' Nyssa was surprised. Her freckles formed a spray across the bridge of her nose, the same colour as her tightly curled hair. 'I've always hated them.'

'They're charming. They make you look healthy. I'm always so pale.'

More than ever, Nyssa was grateful for Rianth's company. She had slept well after being sick on the balcony, and Vendavo had visited her in the morning; but as soon as he was satisfied that she had recovered from her nausea, he had returned to his room and his work, leaving her alone until Rianth rescued her.

'I wish I had your beautiful hair,' Nyssa said with feeling, 'instead of this bird's nest.'

Rianth did not smile. Instead she raised a hand to her head and lifted the hair entirely from her scalp.

Underneath, her real hair was patchy and thin, lying flat on her head. It was like the hair of a baby.

'A side-effect of my illness,' she told Nyssa. 'Khendra says it will grow back when I'm well again.'

Nyssa swallowed, once again at a loss for words. Without the wig, Rianth looked like a plague victim. She opened the top drawer of her dresser.

The drawer was filled with a variety of wigs in different styles and colours. Rianth began taking them out and tossing them on the bed.

'My father had them made,' she told Nyssa. 'I only wear the one that's like my real hair.'

'I'm sorry,' Nyssa said helplessly, staring at them. Blonde, brown, black, braided, curled and bobbed. It was ridiculous. What could Heshezz have been thinking of?

'It's quite all right,' Rianth said. 'I laughed when my father gave me them. He's rather strange at times.' She began rummaging through the wigs. 'Khendra's just as bad. Do you know he keeps a skeleton in his bedroom?'

'A skeleton?'

'A real one. Its bones are fitted together with wires. He claims he has it for anatomical purposes. When I was a child, he used to scare me by sneaking into my room at night with it.'

54

The idea horrified Nyssa. But Rianth was still smiling. Holding up a wig, she said, 'Do you want to try one?'

Before Nyssa could reply, Rianth thrust the wig on Nyssa's head. A long auburn ringlet dangled down over Nyssa's face, and both of them dissolved into laughter.

They experimented with the wigs, trying them all on. There was one which matched Nyssa's own hair almost exactly. Rianth held it up and began to grin.

'Khendra's gone riding,' she told Nyssa. 'I've got an idea.'

Nyssa's bedroom door opened and Khendra entered, a glass of milk in his hand.

'Still asleep?' he said to the mound that lay in the bed, a white sheet drawn up so that only a tuft of auburn hair could be seen.

He pulled back the sheet and recoiled, giving a squeak of horror. The glass fell from his hand, shattering on the floor.

In the bed rested a skeleton with a curly brown wig. Khendra backed away, hands twitching, mouth opening and closing in wordless outrage. Nyssa and Rianth, hidden in the wardrobe and watching him through a crack in the door, began to snigger.

'Surprise!' they shouted, bursting out of the wardrobe.

Khendra backed into the door. He began to splutter, his jowled face turning red. He made to speak, then turned and wrenched open the door, hurrying out.

Nyssa and Rianth collapsed into giggles on the bed.

Dusk had fallen, but the heat of the afternoon still lay heavy over the garden. Nyssa sat in the shallows of a pool, watching Rianth swim slowly through the deeper water. The pool had been set aside for human use, and every morning servants with nets trawled it to remove all other animal life.

Nyssa could not swim herself, but the buoyancy of the water was comforting. She clung to a tuft of reeds, stretching out her legs and wiggling her toes.

Presently she and Rianth climbed out of the water. They were both naked, and it seemed to Nyssa that their bodies were a study in contrasts: hers bulging and sun-browned, Rianth's almost wraith-like in the gloom.

They stretched themselves out on the grass. Tall ferns and bushes screened them from the night patrols.

'How is Vendavo's chimera progressing?' Rianth asked.

Nyssa took a towel and began to rub at the damp edges of her hair.

'I don't know,' she said. 'I haven't seen him since this morning.'

She was hoping he would come to her room tonight and perhaps even sleep with her. But it seemed unlikely. He had not emerged from his room all day, and food left outside his door went uneaten. The drapes were now drawn on the balcony window so that she could not see inside, and she had heard nothing.

'Do you think it will be ready in time?' Rianth asked. 'Wouldn't it be strange to introduce my "mother" to everyone at the ball?'

'I'm sure he won't let you down,' Nyssa replied, hoping that the darkness hid the unease on her face. What would happen if Vendavo *did* succeed in creating a perfect likeness of her?

'The ball will be such fun,' Rianth said, taking her own towel and drying her legs. 'I haven't seen most of my friends for ages. It's a shame you won't be able to dance, Nyssa.'

Her hands were like claws, and her ribs showed taut through her skin.

'There'll be other times,' Nyssa said softly.

Nyssa woke abruptly and felt a pressure beginning to build in her womb.

She steadied herself in the bed, closing her eyes, feeling as if her womb was bulging and rippling. Finally – she did not know how long it took – the pressure ebbed away.

Outside, it was still dark, and all was quiet. Some time passed before the next contraction overtook her. She tried to ride with the discomfort, staring resolutely at the ceiling. Lemon and piebald moths were dotted there, safe for the night from the garden's predators.

Old Ulya, their housekeeper in Veridi-Almar, had told her what to expect, for she had borne eleven children. There was ample time yet, and she had no intention of calling Khendra until it was absolutely necessary. She wasn't going to call anyone, least of all Vendavo, until they could actually do something to help her.

Heavenly host, it was a long ordeal! She drew in a chestful of air, hissed it out slowly. Birds had begun to sing in the garden, and dawn was breaking. Sweat filmed her body, and she had thrown off the bedclothes, only her thin white cotton nightgown covering her. She had found that as the pain returned each time she was able to bear its slowly increasing strength with the same measure of courage. After all, it was necessary, inevitable, productive pain. The contractions were coming much faster and harder now.

Vendavo had been awake all night: she had heard him moving about, and once or twice he had cried out inarticulately. When immersed in his work, he would often go for two or three days without sleep until it was complete. But now she needed him.

The simplest thing would be to call out; but that did not seem right. She waited until a contraction passed before getting out of bed and opening her door.

The house was quiet: even the servants weren't up yet. She crept along to his door, tapped on it. When there was no response, she whispered loudly: 'Vendavo!', and tapped again.

The door opened a head's width and Vendavo peered out. His eyes were red-rimmed, his hair and clothing unkempt. There was an intensity in his eyes, but at the same time they seemed unfocused, registering nothing of what they saw.

'What is it?' he asked.

'The child is coming.'

He did not react. He was plainly distracted. But then he seemed to shake himself before saying, 'Wait here.'

He closed the door in her face. She braced herself against another spasm, pressing both hands flat against the wall.

Vendavo emerged and ushered her back to her room, saying, 'Where's Khendra?'

'I haven't told him yet. I've been waiting until I'm closer to my time.'

He made her get back into bed. Did she want anything? A cup of water? Towels? Something for the pain? Was it bad? Was the baby coming now? What did she want him to do?

'Wake Rianth,' Nyssa said in desperation.

He hurried away.

Another spasm. As it subsided, Rianth appeared.

'Vendavo's gone to fetch Khendra,' she told Nyssa. 'How long have you been having the pains?'

'A few hours, maybe more. I'm sorry, Rianth. I know you're going to be busy today getting everything ready for the ball. I was hoping the baby would wait till after it.'

'Don't be foolish,' Rianth said, raising her head and plumping the pillows underneath. 'If necessary, it will just have to go on without me.'

'You can't –' Nyssa began, but her protest was cut short by another wave of pain.

Presently Khendra scuttled in, Vendavo at his shoulder. He looked bleary and disgruntled, his dressing gown loosely tied around his bulging belly, his hair tousled with sleep.

'Hot water,' he said to Rianth.

She departed to fetch it. Khendra bared Nyssa's belly, while Vendavo hovered in the background. Nyssa understood that his anxiety was not entirely, not even primarily, directed at her.

'You don't have to stay,' she told him.

He glanced at Khendra, then back at her. Nyssa had never seen him quite so agitated.

'I'm going to be some time yet,' she said.

Still he did not move. He looked like a cornered animal.

'Go!' she said, almost shouting it.

He turned and hurried away. Moments later, Rianth arrived with a bowl of hot water and several towels.

'Again,' Khendra ordered. 'Push.'

She heaved and strained, delirious with pain, her body soaked with sweat. Her back felt as if it was going to break, and the spasms were coming so often now that they merged into one continuous agony. How much longer would it go on? All morning she'd laboured, and into the stifling afternoon. Rianth was swabbing her head with a damp towel, while Khendra insisted that the baby was ready to be delivered.

She pushed with each contraction, arching her back to try to get some relief from the pain there. Khendra began to shout, but she was too far gone to hear what he was saying. Then Rianth's face loomed in front of hers.

'It's coming,' she whispered. 'The head's showing. Just a little more.'

Still she didn't quite believe that the baby was going to be delivered. Rianth had insisted on staying with her throughout her labour, turning away a woman servant who had been sent to help Khendra. Nyssa was certain she would not have been able to bear the pain without her.

She pushed hard, and a searing pain attacked her innards.

'Again!' she heard Khendra shouting. 'Again!'

Heavenly host, she was being torn apart! But she had to end the agony somehow. Once more she squeezed, and something seemed to break, a sudden surge of movement.

The pain faded away, and Nyssa thought that at last it was over.

'The head's out,' Rianth whispered.

She felt Khendra's hairy arms brush against the inside of her thighs. She felt the baby turn within her. *Breathe* properly, she told herself. *In. Out.* She could see nothing over the pillow which Khendra had placed across her midriff.

Another surge of pain forced her to bear down. More of the baby slid out. Surely her womb had burst. Surely there was blood everywhere. Another surge. She felt the baby being pulled out of her.

She saw Khendra raise it into his arms. It was bluish-purple, streaked with blood and slime. It made no sound. The cord trailed down to her legs like a withered stalk. Khendra slapped the child sharply on its bottom. Immediately it began to bawl.

Tears were oozing from her eyes. Relief washed through her like a balm, obliterating all pain. She held out her hands for the child. Khendra hesitated, then laid it on her breast.

'A boy,' Rianth said. 'You have a boy.'

Her own eyes were wet. The baby snuggled under Nyssa's chin, its sparse black hair plastered to its flattened scalp. Already its skin was turning from blue to pink. Nyssa kept crying, joyous and relieved. Khendra took a gulp from a bottle of wine which one of the maids had brought to the room.

'Now,' he said, 'let's cut the cord and be done with it.'

Nyssa woke to find Rianth sitting beside the bed. The baby was asleep in a nest of pillows beside her.

'How long have I been sleeping?' she asked.

'Not long.'

But she could tell from the shadows on the balcony that the evening was well advanced. 'You ought to be getting ready for the ball.'

'There's time. The household staff are arranging everything. All I have to do is put my dress on. He's beautiful, Nyssa. He looks just like you.'

'I'm going to call him Leshtu,' Nyssa said. 'At the orphanage they told me it was my father's name.'

Rianth gave a tired smile. The darkness under her eyes was deeper than ever. Nyssa shifted in the bed, felt a soreness at her centre. The sheets had been changed beneath her, she saw, even while she slept.

'Has your father returned yet?' she asked.

Rianth nodded. 'He sends his congratulations.'

'Vendavo?'

'He's still in his room. Do you want me to fetch him?'

'No,' Nyssa said firmly. 'Does he know?'

'Not yet. You said you didn't want him disturbed, and we thought it better to wait until you were awake.'

'Thank you.'

'For what?'

'For everything.'

Rianth reached down and picked up a wicker carrying-basket which she laid on the bed beside Nyssa. It was finely made, with white linen sheets inside.

'I sent one of the maids into Veridi-Almar this morning,' she told Nyssa. 'The dark-skinned one. She loves babies.'

Leshtu was sound asleep in the basket, and Nyssa felt proud that she had managed to breast-feed him without help. The milk flowed easily, collecting at the corners of his lips as he gulped with some strength at her nipple. It was sore now, chafing at her gown, but she felt more a mother than ever. Afterwards she had taken a luxurious bath, washing her hair in lemon-scented water.

She opened the door and crept along to Vendavo's room. Music filtered up from the reception hall below – string instruments and cymbals. Guests had been arriving all evening, and Nyssa had watched their carriages appear through the darkening trees, passing along the winding coachway to pull up outside the house. Lords and ladies in fine silks, young men in smart military uniforms, young women in daring dresses, fleet-footed and high-spirited. Guards were posted everywhere, scrutinizing each new arrival thoroughly.

To her surprise, she saw that Vendavo's door was slightly ajar. She pushed it open, stepped inside.

Oil-lamps burned on a dresser and a bedside table, but the room was empty. It smelt strongly of Vendavo, but she knew he was gone. The bedsheets were tousled, clothes lay cast-off on the floor, a plate of half-eaten cold meats sat on a pillow. Never had a room looked more abandoned.

She wondered if he had already gone down to the ball. Some instinct took her out on to the balcony.

The aviary could be seen clearly, darker somehow than the night itself. Two figures were strolling near it, their backs to her. Vendavo was dressed in cream, and his companion wore a silvery gown which seemed to shine in the darkness. He led her by the arm like a father guiding a young child. They walked towards the ornamental bridge, disappearing behind a stand of trees.

Nyssa returned to her own room and studied herself in the mirror above her dresser. The pink gown fitted her better than she had anticipated. Though exhausted, she was determined to attend the ball: the sight of Vendavo in the garden with the girl was her goad. She picked up the basket, marvelling at Leshtu's lightness, and went out.

Downstairs, two guards were on duty outside the ballroom. They barred her entry, inspecting the basket. She told them who she was – Vendavo's wife. One of them slipped through the doors and presently returned, telling her that she could enter.

A portly Welcomer stood just inside the doors. She asked him not to announce her. Couples were dancing on the floor, while the rest of the guests sat at tables arranged around the ballroom's edge. They sipped wine and nibbled sweetmeats under pendulous lanterns.

Nyssa saw Rianth and her father at a table next to the recess where the musicians were playing. Khendra and Ordeshe were also present, along with a white-haired man she had never seen before.

Nyssa was daunted by the gathering, by the elegance and formality of the guests. But, to her relief, Rianth beamed on seeing her.

'Nyssa!' she said. 'I thought you would be sleeping.'

Ordeshe hastened to take the basket from her. An extra chair was found, and Leshtu, securely bundled up, was put on the floor at her side.

'Isn't he a fine baby?' Rianth said.

Ordeshe and the white-haired man made affirmative noises. Heshezz did not give the child the barest glance. And neither did Khendra, who looked the worse for wine.

Rianth introduced the white-haired man as Almeneris, none other than Jormalu's personal physician. Jormalu himself was not able to attend the ball but had sent the doctor in his stead. At first Nyssa assumed that he and Khendra were close friends, but this did not appear to be the case. Khendra seemed to resent his presence, scowling into his wine and saying little.

Nyssa quickly established that Vendavo had not yet appeared at the ball, and she was relieved that no one expected her to know where he was. She said nothing of what she had seen from the balcony.

Almeneris invited Rianth to dance, and Nyssa watched them slowly spiral across the floor, the other dancers being careful to give them ample room. When she returned to the table, she looked fatigued.

'When was the child born?' Almeneris asked Nyssa.

'A few hours ago,' Nyssa told him.

He frowned. 'As I thought. You're either a very brave or a very foolish young woman. You should be resting.'

Nyssa made light of it, though in fact she longed to lie down, to sleep again. But she was determined to wait until Vendavo appeared.

The music and dancing continued, but Rianth declined further invitations on to the floor. From time to time young men and women approached the table to present their congratulations on her birthday. Some brought small gifts which Rianth placed on the floor under her chair. All the while Heshezz sat motionless in his uniform, staring hard into space.

At length a servant appeared and whispered in his ear. He listened intently before nodding. The servant departed.

Soon afterwards the musicians stopped playing. All the dancers left the floor, and the drone of conversation faded into an expectant murmuring.

'Has he arrived?' Rianth asked her father.

But Heshezz gave her no reply.

The Welcomer called for silence. Then he made to open the doors. In a loud voice he said, 'The artist Vendavo and his latest creation!'

The doors were flung open. In walked Vendavo, the woman in silver on his arm.

The hall was drowned in silence. No one moved. Vendavo, a picture of formality, led the woman forward. She walked slowly but effortlessly, a faint smile on her lips. From a distance she looked the exact image of Rianth. Nyssa gazed in awe as they crossed the floor to Heshezz's table.

Vendavo stopped in front of them. He released the woman's hand and bowed. He did not even glance at Nyssa.

The woman continued smiling, her violet-blue eyes fixed on Heshezz. There was no response from him, not even the flicker of an eyelid. Everything seemed to halt.

This is horrible, Nyssa thought suddenly. She stole a glance at Rianth, who was gazing at the woman with admiration. Almeneris and Ordeshe also looked impressed, while Khendra was slack-jawed with naked incredulity.

Vendavo straightened and said, 'Allow me to present Marael.'

Still Heshezz did not move or speak. There was not a sound anywhere. Then Rianth said, 'Father, isn't it marvellous?'

Immediately it was as if everyone in the ballroom released a breath. Sounds of approval broke out, gained force, and within seconds most of the guests were on their feet, acclaiming the creation. But at the same time many looked uneasy, some aghast; they applauded by rote, as the moment demanded, but to them the chimera-woman was plainly a horror rather than a marvel.

Vendavo turned and bowed low to various sections of his audience. It took a long while for the hubbub to diminish, and throughout it all Marael's pleasing smile scarcely altered. Finally Heshezz turned to the others around the table.

'Gentlemen,' he said, 'would you leave us for a while?'

It was a demand rather than a request. Almeneris and Khendra were quick to withdraw. Ordeshe lingered, sitting close to Rianth.

'You, too,' Heshezz said brusquely.

Nyssa was certain she would also be asked to leave. But Heshezz continued to ignore her. When Ordeshe was gone, he motioned to the empty chairs.

'Be seated,' he told Vendavo and his companion.

All eyes were still on the woman. Without Vendavo's help, she sat down effortlessly. Her eyelids blinked, her dark hair shone, there were even smile-lines at the corners of her mouth. She looked utterly real, and Nyssa found it hard to believe that she was a creature wrested from nothingness by the power of her husband's mind.

'Does she speak?' Heshezz asked.

'Alas, no,' replied Vendavo. 'That was beyond my powers. But she'll listen to you and do whatever you say.'

Still Heshezz did not betray what he thought of her. But Rianth seemed delighted.

'Did my mother really look like that?' she asked.

Her father merely grunted. Nyssa suddenly felt a deep pity for Rianth; it was plain she hadn't recognized the chimera as a replica of herself. And yet this was not entirely surprising. Vendavo had been unable to resist giving Marael's figure a proper fullness, perhaps basing her on a completely healthy Rianth. Her features, too, were slightly softer, her skin somewhat darker, her lips a deeper pink. And while Vendavo had obviously done everything in his power to make her movements perfectly natural, they did tend to the statuesque when carefully observed: she sat too straight-backed in her chair, and when she turned her head, her shoulders did not move. It was these small features which finally convinced Nyssa that Marael was indeed a chimera and not a real human lookalike of Rianth.

Heshezz gave a signal, and the musicians began playing again. Gradually couples began to drift out on to the floor. More and more joined them as they realized they could pass near the table and see the woman at close quarters.

Rianth, meanwhile, could not hide her delight.

'I'm pleased to meet you,' she said to Marael.

The woman's smile broadened.

'Do you eat?' Rianth asked, offering her a dish of sugared dates.

Marael stared at it but did not lift a hand.

'No,' Vendavo said. 'She can't eat or drink, and has no need of either. You must remember that even I couldn't create a human being with all the qualities that make us human. She has an appearance of life – perhaps even life itself – but it's not the same as ours. Of course it pleases me that you should think of her as a real person –'

'How long will she last?' Heshezz asked, not taking his eyes off her.

'That I can't judge,' Vendavo replied. 'But I'd be surprised if it's less than a man's lifetime.'

Marael was now returning the curious glances of the dancers who swayed by. She seemed to relish their attention, raising a hand to stroke her hair. The movement seemed at once calculated and instinctive. Her eyes shone under the lantern light. They gave a surface appearance of vitality, but there was something flat and hard about them; they lacked real expressiveness. The more Nyssa studied her, the easier she found it to believe that she was a magnificent creation but far from truly human.

'Can she understand us?' Heshezz asked.

Vendavo shook his head slowly. 'My greatest difficulty wasn't in reproducing the physical form but in giving her a proper semblance of human behaviour. She'll respond to simple instructions or react to the tone of your voice, but *understanding* – that isn't the question. You can't expect her to be as rounded and complex as a real human being. Not in any way. Think of her as a well-trained pet, or a bird that talks when you whistle. You may take her and do what you want with her – within the limits of her physique, of course.'

Marael was watching Vendavo as he spoke. Her expression did not alter a fraction.

'That's sad,' Rianth said. 'You're saying she has no life of her own.'

Again Vendavo shook his head. 'You mustn't misunderstand me – I'm not saying that at all. But whatever life she has is not the same as ours, and you mustn't make the mistake of thinking it is. She can survive quite independently of any of us, but it would be a blank, empty existence. She needs the stimulus of real people around her if she's to give of her best.'

Nyssa had been patient, wanting to give Vendavo ample time to relish the admiration that was his due. But enough was enough.

'We have a son,' she said sharply. Then, reaching down, she hauled up the wicker basket and placed it on the centre of the table, pushing aside the cups and plates and wine bottles, damned if she would care whether Heshezz or anyone else disapproved.

Vendavo gazed down at the still-sleeping child. He looked astounded, as if no one had told him it had been born.

'Nyssa,' he whispered. 'Forgive me.'

He reached into the basket and picked up the child. Immediately it awoke and peered at him with wide blue eyes which matched his own.

'I've named him Leshtu,' she said.

Vendavo hardly seemed to hear her. He stroked his son's cheek with his forefinger. Its mouth puckered, began to open and close. Vendavo offered the tip of his little finger. Leshtu began to suck eagerly.

Marael looked on, almost as if she understood what was happening. Now there seemed to be a real depth in her eyes. And yet it was not, Nyssa realized, a depth of understanding but simply a *sucking in* of sights. She was like a flower that opened to take in the sunlight – instinctively, unknowingly.

Vendavo held the baby awkwardly in his arms, its head lolling.

'He's beautiful,' he told Nyssa. 'Leshtu. My little Leshtu. It suits him.'

'Does she dance?' Heshezz asked.

Vendavo looked up. Heshezz was still intent on Marael.

66

'If you lead her,' Vendavo said, 'she'll follow.'

Heshezz turned to Rianth. 'Take her on to the floor.'

Rianth looked startled. She shook her head.

'I'll take her,' said a voice.

It was Ordeshe, who had approached the table once more. He was gazing at Marael with outright admiration.

'Leave us!' Heshezz told him savagely.

Ordeshe swiftly withdrew.

'Take her,' Heshezz said again to Rianth. 'I want to talk to Vendavo.'

Reluctantly Rianth rose. She stretched out a hand to the woman.

Marael reached up and clasped it, rising from her chair. She allowed Rianth to lead her forward on to the ballroom floor. Rianth took both her hands, and they spiralled away, watched by every other dancer.

'It's not her,' Heshezz said to Vendavo.

Vendavo freed his fingers from Leshtu's mouth. He smiled.

'Don't you think so?' he said.

'She *resembles* my daughter, but it's not her.'

Vendavo handed the baby across to Nyssa. 'I'm sorry she fails to please you. To me, she is your daughter, or at least certain aspects of her. You may remember I told you at the start that a perfect likeness which would satisfy everyone wouldn't be possible. Each of us sees things with different eyes.'

'Even my daughter doesn't recognize her as herself.'

'That's a good thing, I would have thought. And not entirely surprising. Who ever sees themselves as others do?'

'Nevertheless,' Heshezz went on as if he hadn't spoken, 'you have, by all accounts, worked hard to fashion the chimera according to my requirements. And the result is quite remarkable in its way – a creature one might almost think is alive. You may consider the commission discharged.'

Only now did Vendavo begin to look a little thwarted. He sat down.

'Will she suffice as a replacement for your daughter?' he asked.

'Don't be fatuous,' Heshezz replied. 'If the likeness had been perfect, it could never have done that.'

Nyssa loosened the front of her dress and put Leshtu to her

breast. To Heshezz, she was invisible. Both he and Vendavo were watching Rianth and Marael on the floor. Rianth was a practised dancer, and Marael mimicked her steps almost exactly, the perfect partner. They were like twins, joined fast to one another, Marael the more vital of the two.

Vendavo glanced ruefully at Nyssa. She knew she should still be angry with him, but she was never able to brood or bear grudges. When he reached across the table for her hand, she let him take it.

The dance ended. As Rianth and Marael disengaged, their audience began to applaud. Then Ordeshe stepped out of the crowd to take Marael's hand.

'I'd destroy the world for her if it would help,' Heshezz muttered.

He was not addressing either of them directly. His eyes were shadowed under the lantern, his jaw set hard. A hot pain shot down between Nyssa's legs, and Leshtu almost slipped from her arms. Neither Vendavo nor Heshezz noticed.

Rianth returned to the table, looking flustered and exhausted.

'She's cold,' she said to Vendavo. 'Her skin is cold.'

'It's as warm as the air,' he replied. 'It only feels cold compared with real human skin. She has no blood inside her, you must remember.'

'It was like dancing with a corpse – Nyssa, what's the matter?'

Something hot and wet was gushing out from between her legs, and she could no longer hide the pain she felt.

'Take the baby,' she said to Rianth.

But it was Vendavo who plucked the child from her breast. She managed to raise herself, saw blood staining her skirt. Even Heshezz was on his feet, motioning to someone.

Khendra and Almeneris appeared. All the strength rushed out of her legs. But the two doctors caught her by the arms and began shepherding her away. The last thing she saw was Marael dancing with Ordeshe, still smiling vacantly . . .

Throughout the night she kept surfacing from a black sleep, catching glimpses of faces and hearing fragments of conversation. Almeneris was leaning over her, Rianth and Vendavo were there, looking concerned, the baby was crying. Vendavo kept telling her not to worry, she was in good hands, everything necessary was being done. Rapidly she would sink down into sleep again.

Finally she woke knowing that she had slept longer and more restfully than before. It was morning, and a middle-aged woman was sitting by her bedside in the sunlit room. The wicker basket sat on a table next to her.

'Leshtu,' Nyssa murmured.

The woman lifted the sleeping child out of the basket and laid him on her breast. Leshtu snuggled, small and warm, against the crook of her neck without waking. The woman slipped out, and presently Almeneris appeared. Vendavo was at his side.

'Am I dying?' Nyssa asked.

Almeneris gave a short laugh. 'Not at all. It was a haemorrhage, and you lost blood – a consequence of the after-birth not having been properly removed.' He put a hand to her brow. 'You were also foolish to over-tax yourself by going to the ball so soon after giving birth. But you're young and healthy, and you may be assured that you'll bear many more children. All that's needed now is several days of complete rest.'

Vendavo came forward and took her hand under the sheet. He squeezed it fiercely.

'Can we go home?' she asked him.

He looked at the doctor.

'That may well be the wisest thing,' Almeneris said. 'But you must travel slowly, in a comfortable coach.'

'It was Khendra's fault,' Vendavo told her. 'He was incompetent.'

Almeneris peered closely at her eyes. 'Console yourselves with the fact that you won't have him tending you again.' He nodded as if satisfied. 'I'll prescribe a tonic before you leave.'

He went out, closing the door behind him.

Vendavo stroked her hair.

'We'll leave today,' he said. 'I'll make the arrangements.'

He had had a fright, that was plain. It was a relief to be alone with him again. But before she could tell him as much, he said, 'I've got something for you.'

He went out, returning shortly with an ornament held carefully in both hands. He set it down on the table.

No taller than a candle, it was a still-life chimera of a lustrous green and blue hummingbird poised in the act of taking nectar from the centre of a mottled white orchid. The green stem of the flower flattened into a base which supported the whole creation. The details, the proportions, the colours – all were perfect.

'It's beautiful,' Nyssa said, hugging the baby to her.

Silence fell. Vendavo stared toward the balcony. For once, he seemed at a loss for words.

'Where's Marael?' Nyssa asked.

'Downstairs.'

'Did she enjoy the party?'

'You mustn't give her human qualities she doesn't possess, Nyssa. Enjoyment isn't something she's capable of – she just responds to whatever stimulus is given her. Apparently she danced all night. Everyone in the ballroom wanted to be her partner, though few, I gather, danced with her more than once. The coldness of her skin. I always thought that might be a problem.'

'Still, you must be very proud.'

He made a movement which seemed to combine a nod and a shrug. 'I think it was worth doing. But there's always more to be done, different things. She isn't mine any more.'

'Does she need to sleep?'

He shook his head. 'She doesn't need anything except the acknowledgement of her existence.'

He reached forward and turned the chimera, as if wanting to present her with a different view of it. The arrangement of the flower's petals echoed the spread of the bird's wings and tail, while the purple spots on its petals were reflected in the bird's mottled breast.

Nyssa steeled herself. 'Could a man make love to her?'

'No,' Vendavo said. 'Not in a sexual way. If they tried, she wouldn't stop them, but nothing could be consummated. I deliberately didn't design that feature into her.'

'Because you knew men would try?'

'Perhaps.'

'Isn't that what they always want?'

'Not always. Often, I'll admit. To satisfy a hunger or slake a thirst. That's all it is, Nyssa.'

70

He had such eyes; they could make you believe almost any lie.

The coach stood outside the main entrance to the house, four docile grey mares at its front. Nyssa and Rianth sat in the shade of the verandah, Leshtu asleep in Rianth's arms.

'He seems a very peaceful child,' she remarked.

'If he had been a girl,' Nyssa said, 'I would have named him after you.'

Rianth smiled. She was paler than ever, her eyes sunken, drained by the long night and all its drama.

'Where's Ordeshe?' Nyssa asked.

'He's taken Marael to the aviary to show her the birds. Do you want to see them before you go?'

'No,' Nyssa said, rather too firmly and hastily. She particularly had no desire to see Marael. But Rianth did not pursue the matter. Apparently Ordeshe had danced with Marael half the night, and such was the interest in her that most guests had not left until dawn.

'Where's Khendra?' Nyssa asked. The doctor had not been in evidence all morning.

'I don't know,' Rianth replied. 'My father's angry with him about something. Probably about the way he bungled your labour. I expect he's sleeping off a surfeit of wine in his room.'

A servant appeared and loaded their case on to the coach. Birds called to one another from the trees. It was a cooler day, veiled with cloud.

Vendavo emerged from the house, his cloak draped over one shoulder. The hummingbird chimera had been wrapped in soft paper, then put into a box. He held it carefully in both hands.

'Are you ready?' he said to Nyssa.

She nodded. Rianth passed Leshtu to her and she laid him in the basket.

'Would you like to see Marael before you leave?' Rianth asked Vendavo.

'That's not necessary,' he replied. 'She's yours now. I have very little sentimental attachment to my creations.'

They crossed to the coach. A servant took the basket and

71

loaded it inside. Nyssa hesitated, not knowing what to say to Rianth.

'I'm sorry my father couldn't be here to see you off,' Rianth remarked. 'I'm afraid he was called away early this morning.'

'Ah,' said Vendavo. 'Well, no matter. We're very grateful for your hospitality.'

'He did ask that I enquire about one thing.' Rianth hesitated. 'Is it possible . . . that is, can Marael be hurt in any way?'

'She feels no pain,' Vendavo said. 'You could plunge a knife into her heart, feed her poison, and it would have no effect. Of course she can be mutilated or destroyed by burning or some other means of degrading the human body, but she has no feeling. None. If tortured, she won't protest. Whatever marks are made on her body will not, of course, heal. But she will never bleed.'

It was as if he had rehearsed the answer well in advance. Without further ado, he swung himself up into the carriage.

Rianth looked distraught. 'I've offended him. I didn't mean to suggest that my father meant her any harm.'

'Of course not,' Nyssa said. 'He's tired, drained. I think we all need a rest.'

Inside the carriage, Leshtu began to cry.

'I must go,' Nyssa said.

'I'm going to miss you,' Rianth told her.

Nyssa hugged her as fiercely as her frail figure would allow. An odour of medicinal staleness clung to the hair of her wig.

'Perhaps we can come and see you again,' Nyssa said.

'Yes. Don't leave it too long.'

5

Drifting veils of winter rain washed the carriage as it ploughed along the muddy track. Nyssa peeked out the window and saw the line of cypresses in the grey distance.

'We'll soon be there,' she announced.

Vendavo said nothing. He sat hunched in his fur-fringed cloak, Leshtu wriggling in his lap. He had been in a poor humour since they were forced to return from their mountain retreat to attend the funeral in Veridi-Almar. The bad weather had done nothing to improve his mood.

Nyssa took Leshtu from him, letting the child snatch at her hair. The invitation to the house had been passed on to her by one of Heshezz's servants during the cremation, and Nyssa had insisted they accept it. The funeral itself was a full state occasion, conducted on a bright and bitter day. She had glimpsed Jormalu, bundled up in brown furs in the back of an open carriage, and Almeneris was also present, though he had not recognized her. Vendavo, never at ease where death was concerned, behaved with his usual courtliness while in the public eye; but privately he did not cease complaining about having to endure the cold. Inside the temple it was particularly bitter, their breath clouding the sanctified air. She suspected that the people who had lingered around the flaming pyre-dish afterwards had done so as much for warmth as respect.

The carriage jolted and squelched through the mud; it was the most hostile winter in years. Leshtu burped, depositing a gobbet of milk on the shoulder of her cloak. She wiped it away with a handkerchief. Her feet were numb with the cold.

Several soldiers were on duty outside the gate, huddled miserably under hooded cloaks. They stopped the coach and peered inside. The driver had already announced them, and they were not delayed. Hoofs crunched on gravel as they passed through the gates.

The garden drooped with water and decay. Trees hung low, sodden leaves strewed the lawns, the flowerbeds were bedraggled and colourless. It was silent, not a bird singing, none even in sight. Everything was a drab soaked green.

Two manservants stood under the verandah with umbrellas. Quickly they were ushered inside.

Ordeshe was waiting in the hall. After greeting them somewhat stiffly, he took their cloaks, told a servant to fetch hot drinks, then led them directly upstairs.

A wood fire burned in the bedroom and Rianth lay asleep, swamped by white pillows and sheets. She wore no wig, and her head had been shaved. As Ordeshe closed the door behind them, she stirred and opened her eyes.

'Nyssa,' she said after a moment.

Nyssa handed Leshtu to Vendavo, then went across and embraced her.

'It's good to see you,' Rianth murmured. 'I'm glad you came.'

She was as frail as ever, and the odour of sickness still clung to her.

'Can I hold him?' she asked, gazing at Leshtu.

Vendavo handed the child over while Ordeshe arranged chairs at the bedside. It was unlike Leshtu to remain docile for long, but he seemed to settle happily in Rianth's arms, peering up at her face with a depthless scrutiny.

'How old is he now?' she asked.

'Almost five months,' Nyssa said.

'Five months. It *has* been a long time.'

She held out a finger, and he took it in his hand.

'How are you feeling?' Nyssa asked.

Rianth lay back against the pillows. 'On the road to recovery, Almeneris says. I was much worse to begin with, but apparently that's because the poison is now expelling itself from my body. In a month or two I'll be able to get up.'

'Was Khendra really trying to kill you?'

'My father thought he was, and that sealed his fate. Because of what had happened to you, Almeneris examined me after you left, and then had Khendra questioned about his milk. Apparently there had always been friction between them, and he seized on the opportunity of exposing Khendra's incompetence. Khendra was using some kind of poisonous root or fungus in it – small amounts, but enough to make you ill if taken for long enough. I was, in fact, becoming steadily more ill because of it.'

'Did Khendra ever admit anything?'

'I doubt that he had the opportunity. I never saw him again after the night of the ball. No one did. My father had him swiftly removed, and, I suspect, swiftly put out of his misery. He was convinced that Khendra was not only trying to kill me but had also killed my mother.'

'But why? Why should he want to kill you?'

'My father had many enemies, and he told me that Khendra was a member of a rebel group which is dedicated to the overthrow of the Hierarchy. Apparently they also specialize

74

in murdering members of the ruling families. But Khendra was no assassin. After all, he gave you some of his milk too, and I can't see why he'd want to poison you, can you?' She drew in a long, slow breath. 'I think he was just a poor physician. But my father had to strike out at something.'

A servant entered with a tray holding a selection of hot cordials. Rianth took nothing. Leshtu continued to sit contentedly in her arms. Without any hair whatsoever, she closely resembled her father. If anything, she looked sicker than before.

'It must be sad for you,' Nyssa said, 'knowing that you'll soon be restored to health but have lost your father.'

Rianth gave a wan smile. 'He always said he would never die in his bed. He had too many enemies, and there had been several attempts on his life over the years. But I didn't expect a crone to put an end to him with a butcher's knife.'

Heshezz had died during a parade to celebrate the anniversary of the founding of Veridi-Almar. While leading a cavalry procession down a street, he had been pulled from his horse by an old woman who darted from the crowd and plunged a meat-cleaver into his neck. Rianth had sent Nyssa a letter at her mountain retreat, saying that she was too ill to attend the funeral herself and asking Nyssa to go in her stead.

Rianth's eyes shone with tears. 'Did you know he was responsible for the deaths of thousands? I sometimes think perhaps he was glad when the crone ended it for him. He never really got over losing my mother, never really knew how to love anyone but her.'

'He loved you,' Nyssa said.

She seemed to consider it. 'I suppose he did, in his way. I certainly think he wanted to make me in my mother's image. And Marael, of course, in mine.'

So she knew. Nyssa glanced at Vendavo, but his face gave nothing away. At times, his self-possession amazed her.

'Do you want to see her?' Rianth said. 'She's in the aviary. Ordeshe will take you.'

Now Vendavo did look uneasy. 'There's no need,' he said.

'But you must! Ordeshe tells me she loves it there with all the plants and birds. He's been wonderful, keeping the whole estate going while I've been bedridden. I don't know how I would have managed without him.'

Ordeshe seemed abashed by her compliments. He also appeared less than enthusiastic about the prospect of taking them to Marael. But Rianth was insistent, telling them that they should all go so that she could have some time alone with Leshtu.

Downstairs, Ordeshe collected two umbrellas before leading them outside. By now, his discomfort was obvious.

'Is she dying?' Nyssa said on an intuition.

'We don't know,' Ordeshe told her. 'It's too early to say. The poison was well established in her, and we can't be certain of recovery.'

Huddling under the umbrellas, they strode across the sodden grass.

'I've had to keep things from her,' Ordeshe said. 'She doesn't know that much of her father's wealth was confiscated by Jormalu after his death. That's why the garden has suffered so badly – we can't afford the servants to maintain it any longer.'

'But I thought Heshezz was the Hierarch's uncle.'

'Jormalu needs money to finance his bridge over the Raimus. That need overrides even blood ties.'

Ordeshe hurried on, as if to flee from his own words, which might be thought treasonous.

The aviary was dark under the iron-grey sky, and Nyssa's imagination began to run riot. She was suddenly convinced that terrible things had been done to Marael, that they would find her disfigured, limbless or simply reduced to squalor. The very wretchedness of the garden did not bode well: dead leaves coated everything, a broken branch hung from a tree, the corpse of an ibis drifted in one of the lily ponds. All manner of rumours and tales about Marael had reached them in the mountains long before the funeral.

Ordeshe opened the aviary door. Nyssa was surprised to find herself engulfed in hot moist air: she had expected coldness, death. Ordeshe led them into the heart of the aviary, calling out Marael's name. Suddenly she appeared.

Nyssa did not recognize her immediately, for her hair was now blonde. She had violet lips, painted eyes, and her face had been lightened with powder after the prevailing fashion in Veridi-Almar. Her dress was of the sheerest white cotton through which the nipples of her breasts showed. It had dark smears all over it.

76

'She tends the fires here,' Ordeshe said, shame-faced. 'Rianth doesn't know. She seems to like it here, and I couldn't have kept the aviary going without her.'

Marael, on seeing them, had begun to smile, though there was no apparent recognition in her face at the sight of Vendavo. Tiny green seeds were flecked in her hair. She looked absurd, like a garish life-sized doll.

'Marael,' Ordeshe said, 'this is your creator, Vendavo. Do you remember him?'

Her smile broadened, but there was nothing behind her violet eyes.

'I believe she enjoys the company of the birds and the flowers,' Ordeshe was saying, smothering his embarrassment with words. 'They're exotic creatures just like her.'

'What's happened to her hair?' Vendavo asked evenly. He stood his distance from Marael.

'She wears Rianth's wigs now. Different ones for different occasions. Different dresses, too. I do try to look after her. Of course she gets dusty and untidy in here, but I bathe her and attend completely to her appearance before . . .' His words faltered.

'Before you rent her out,' Vendavo said.

Ordeshe looked helpless. He nodded.

So the rumours were true. After Marael's creation, a variety of other artists in Veridi-Almar had begun fashioning human replicas as escorts and playthings for the nobility and the rich. Nyssa had not seen any of them, but apparently none were remotely as accomplished as Marael. Vendavo too had received many requests for similar creations, but he flatly refused all such commissions. He was working on a series of semi-abstract creations, reproducing complex natural patterns – a tangle of undergrowth, lichens on rock, sunlight on water. To escape the demands for more Maraels, he, Nyssa and Leshtu had departed the city for a remote village in the western mountains, returning only when the news of Heshezz's funeral reached them. By this time, Jormalu had reimposed the ban on creating human-like chimeras and banished those that did exist from the public eye. But Marael in particular still fascinated many people, and word had reached them that visitors to Heshezz's house were charged a fee to enjoy the pleasure of her company.

77

'I can't excuse it,' Ordeshe was saying. 'All I can say is that it's a means of raising money for the upkeep of the estate. And no harm comes to her. She seems to enjoy it.'

Marael was watching his lips as he spoke. She looked as if she was awaiting an invitation to dance.

'I don't think Rianth would forgive me if she knew,' Ordeshe remarked. 'We're going to be married in the spring, if she's well enough.'

Nyssa did not know what to make of him. Initially he had struck her as somewhat insincere in his courtship of Rianth, but there was something about his present honesty which was disarming. Assuming, of course, that he *was* being honest.

As for Marael, she was by her very nature an utter victim of circumstances. At one point a tiny insect landed on a broad leaf, and she raised her hand to try to touch it. It was tempting to see in the gesture proof that Marael had an inner life of her own; but Nyssa knew that it was dangerous to yield to such a temptation. She pitied Marael because she was simply a tool for the amusement of others; but pity did not make her human. Still, it was profoundly sad. Even Vendavo, her creator, had no special affection for her; far from it: he was uncomfortable in her presence and had not actually acknowledged her in any direct way.

'Did you know,' he said to Ordeshe, 'that many inferior artists are now secretly creating human creatures for illicit brothels?'

'I've heard it said,' Ordeshe admitted.

'Apparently their skins are like dough, their eyes like raisins, and they shamble like cows.' He smiled bitterly. 'Thus we set an example for others to follow.'

So saying, he turned on his heels and began striding towards the door.

Ordeshe hesitated for only a moment before pursuing him.

Marael continued to stand there, without impatience or expectation. Nyssa wanted to say something to her, to explain, question, comfort – anything. But she knew it would be absurd. Even so, she reached forward and kissed her lightly on her cheek – her cold cheek – and whispered 'Goodbye' before hurrying out.

Vendavo and Ordeshe were standing outside in the rain, their umbrellas still furled.

'The severe weather has all but destroyed the garden,' Ordeshe was saying. 'Most of the birds and many of the plants are dead. I would dearly love to have it restored to its old splendour by the time Rianth is well again, but it's simply beyond my means. That's why I was wondering whether perhaps as a favour to Rianth you might undertake an ambitious creation for her.'

Vendavo was eyeing him as if he could not credit his presumption.

'It would be a unique garden – a garden filled with birds and flowers and trees that do not exist anywhere else. A garden that would not need tending, whose living things would be immune to frost or rain or drought. A garden that would exist as a living memorial to its creator. A *chimera*-garden, fashioned by an artist who can outmatch Nature herself.'

The rain poured down, but both men were oblivious of it. Vendavo no longer looked incredulous. He was thinking.

Nyssa felt as if a web of ensnarement was closing over them once more. She and Leshtu would be confined to the house all winter with a dying Rianth while her husband laboured in the garden and Marael entertained guests. There would be more lies and deceit for the only person there that she could call a friend . . .

She did not want to be parted from Leshtu a moment longer. Snatching an umbrella from Vendavo's hand, she hurried towards the house.

Cursing and lashing his whip, the coachman bullied the horses through a particularly deep slough. Ahead, Nyssa could see the outskirts of Veridi-Almar on the horizon. The sight pleased her enormously.

She held Leshtu up to the window.

'Why did you refuse him?' she asked. 'I know you wanted to do it.'

'It would be an interesting commission, in theory,' Vendavo agreed.

'Was it because he couldn't pay you?'

'Not entirely. I'm sure we could have negotiated a suitable fee of some sort.'

'Was it because of what Ordeshe has done to Marael?'

'The man has no taste. What did you expect?'

'And that's why you turned him down?'

'Of course.'

She didn't believe him. She said, 'I don't understand why you're so . . . so *remote* towards Marael.'

He shook his head. 'I've told you before – I'm not attached to my creations. Not even her.' He paused, watching Leshtu strain to haul himself up on to the window sill. 'We have to be careful, Nyssa. You know that the priesthood disapprove strongly of human-like creations. And they have Jormalu's ear. It's safer for us if I don't associate myself with her any longer. Also, I knew you didn't want me to do it.'

It was quite unlike him to take her feelings into account as far as his art was concerned.

'It would have been an interesting challenge for you,' she said.

'I don't deny it.'

Like a conjurer, he suddenly flexed his fingers, and a tiny ball blinked into existence, glimmering gold and red and blue. He put it in front of Leshtu to distract him from the window. The ball was soft, and Leshtu immediately pressed it to his mouth.

'In any case,' Vendavo said softly, 'the opportunity isn't entirely lost.'

'What do you mean?'

'The bad weather will have ruined gardens everywhere.'

Nyssa waited. Vendavo hoisted Leshtu on to his knee.

'We can't afford to be out of favour, Nyssa, otherwise this little one will have no bread for his belly. A gesture is needed.'

Leshtu's ball was already forgotten, his mind's eye filled with something new.

'They tell me Jormalu is fond of greenery.' He gave her a perfect smile. 'Come the spring, he might welcome entirely new palace gardens.'

3

The Bridge

The air was alive with a flurry of unseen chimeras. Vendavo stood motionless at the centre of the stable, dusty sunlight slanting in through a broken shutter, the air rank with the smell of horses, even though the beasts had been removed days before. He closed his eyes, his mind filling with visions of barbarians – bearded and scarred men, red-eyed and yellow-toothed, lips cracked and bearskins muddy as they rode across an empty plain under a lowering sky. He could smell their sweat, their foul breath, feel the wind on their faces and the pounding of their horses' hoofs beneath them.

The chimeras pressed in more strongly, filling his head with a babble of whispers, imploring him to fashion them. He felt as if he were buffeted by winds, as if he stood on a mountaintop in an exhilarating gale. Grinning, he resisted their pressure, focusing on a rider at the head of the pack, a black-bearded man with piercing eyes and huge hands which whiplashed the leather reins across the neck of his mount. A thick scar split his right cheek, half his ear was missing and his nostrils were caked with blood. Yes, this one would be the legendary warlord who had swept down from the north, conquering Veridi-Almar and founding a dynasty.

There was a polite cough.

Instantly he let his vision dissipate. And instantly the chimeras retreated, their susurrus diminishing to a murmur.

Mersulis stood patiently, a slim figure in a tight black tunic, her indulgent smile a white arc in an ebony face. Her expression was one of polite boredom; as far as she was concerned, the stable had continued utterly silent and empty apart from the two of them.

'Will it suffice?' she asked.

'Indeed,' said Vendavo. 'It's ideal.'

Mersulis stared disapprovingly at the straw-strewn cobbles and empty stalls. 'Rather bare and lacking in creature comforts, I'd have thought.'

'The space and solitude are exactly what I need.'

'You've told no one about the commission?'

'No.'

'Not even your wife?'

'I explained that I had important work to do, that's all.'

'Good.' Mersulis tapped the heel of her boot against the cobbles. 'Will you be sleeping here?'

Vendavo shook his head. 'My new-born daughter is sick, and I may be needed at home. I'll come before dawn and leave after sunset.'

'Be sure you carry your pass. The military have orders to arrest anyone on the streets after curfew without one. Even you.'

She began striding towards the door. Her cropped hair accentuated her long neck, the sweep of her shoulders. She looked more like the mistress of some exotic brothel than the third wife of the Hierarch. He followed her to the door.

'You realize you have ten days at most?'

He shrugged. 'It will be time enough.'

They stepped outside into the blinding sunlight. Four soldiers in the green uniform of Jormalu's personal guard stood at the head of the alleyway which led to the stable. Like Mersulis, they were all dark-skinned Southerners. Mersulis handed Vendavo the key to the stable door.

'Do you have any message for the Hierarch?' she asked.

Vendavo was prepared for the question.

'Tell him he can have complete confidence in me,' he replied.

The sun hung low and red over the city as Ethoam hurried from the widow Bila's hut. He was late, having lingered too long at her bedside, trying to feed her thin soup and engage her in talk which would make her forget, however briefly, her sickness. He had succeeded in neither, because she was too sunk in pain. Her ulcerated legs gave off the stink of death which made her heavily shaded room even more oppressive. Ethoam was ashamed of the relief he had felt on finally escaping into the street.

There was a stitch in his side, and sweat was trickling down his back under his robes. He passed a butcher's shop which had been gutted during the riots in spring over the increase in food prices. Three months on, the foot patrols of Jormalu's soldiers remained ever-present on the streets.

The temple was a humble ochre-domed building close to the north bank of the Raimus. Just downriver was Jormalu's bridge, a soaring pillared arch of oatmeal stone. Gulls had already found nesting places on its parapets and ledges. Over twenty years in the building, it was soon to be opened by the Hierarch.

Nisbisi, the priestess, was standing just inside the arched door, placing a silver incense holder on a plinth. A stickler for punctuality, she frowned at him as he entered. Two novices in white were busy at the altar, arranging flowers for the evening devotionals.

Ethoam's cubicle was situated behind the altar, and he was relieved to see that only three petitioners sat waiting. The last of them was Tilarwa, and she smiled at him as he passed by.

The cubicle was small and windowless, a single candle burning in a bracket above his chair. Ethoam plumped the cushion at his feet before settling himself in the chair, adjusting his maroon robes over his ample belly. The first of the petitioners entered and knelt in front of him on the cushion.

Ethoam often felt that he was an utter fraud, and never more so than when he undertook his formal duties as a Comforter within the temple itself. The man before him, a smallholder, explained that he had lost half his pigs to swine fever and was threatened with ruin. What could he do? Ethoam went through the ritual of telling him to offer prayers to the Supreme Spirit and practise good works in the hope that his fortunes would improve. The advice sounded fatuous even to him, and the man only grudgingly dropped a handful of coins into the collection box before departing. The second petitioner, a middle-aged woman, was engaged in a long-standing quarrel with her sister over the possession of an ornamental mirror left to them by their father. He had promised it to her on his deathbed, the woman claimed, but her sister refused to accept this. How could she make her see reason? Ethoam sighed as if in contemplation, recalling the same woman on a previous visit fretting over the ownership of the olives on a tree which overhung her garden. He suggested she tell her sister she had sought his advice and that he would be pleased if she too could visit him so that the matter could be fully explored. The woman looked pleased, scarcely

83

listening, it seemed to him, as he also suggested a small donation to a charitable cause and quoted a pertinent passage from a holy text about the virtues of giving rather than receiving. As always, when he adjudicated in matters of material possession, Ethoam felt more like a lawyer than a spiritual counsellor.

The woman left, and Ethoam allowed himself a discreet belch. Before he had been ordained, he had always imagined that Comforters dealt constantly with matters of holiness and penitence, with questions of good and evil, life and death, salvation and damnation. But the temples catered chiefly to the comfortable and well-off, lulling them with their rituals, pandering to their prejudices and petty jealousies while the poor were left to rot in their hovels.

The curtain drew back, and Tilarwa stepped inside.

'You look as sour as a lemon,' she announced.

Ethoam smiled. At nineteen, she was eleven years his junior, yet she showed him no deference whatsoever. She wore a faded olive-green dress which hung on her slender body, and her arms and face were grimy. She made no move to kneel in front of him.

'What ails you today, my child?' he asked with mock formality.

'Nothing,' she said bluntly. 'I came in off the streets because it was cooler. Would you rather I find something to complain about?'

He shook his head, amused and somewhat in awe of her. She had first come to him in the spring to complain that her father wanted to marry her to a man she despised, an undertaker three times her age with no teeth in his head. Ethoam advised her to resist the betrothal if she felt she could never be a dutiful wife to the man, and he also offered to speak to her father. But this had not proved necessary, because when she next came to the cubicle it was to inform him that the undertaker had abandoned his courtship after she flatly refused to marry him. Her left eye was bruised as if from a blow, but she made light of it, dismissing it as an accident.

Ethoam did not flatter himself that he had persuaded her to reject the undertaker, for it seemed to him that she was a strong-willed young woman who had already made up her mind before visiting him. She had never spoken of the matter again, even though she became a regular caller at his cubicle, often for no other apparent reason than to pass the time of day. Her father, a widower, was a tanner, and she was an only child.

Today she seemed somewhat subdued, watching him but saying nothing. Ethoam shifted in his seat, feeling self-conscious.

'Is there something you want to tell me?' he said finally.

'No. Is it against the law for me to come here for no reason?'

'Of course not. It's simply my duty to ask.'

'Why have you never married?'

Her sudden conversational forays always unsettled him, more than ever in this instance. He considered carefully before saying, 'Not many women want to be the wife of a Comforter.'

'Are you celibate?'

Her bluntness seemed artless rather than rude, and he could not bring himself to chastise her – or to refuse to answer her question.

'I don't visit whores, if that's what you mean.' She opened her mouth to say something, but Ethoam hurried on: 'There were women once, before I became a Comforter. Now my duties don't permit me the luxury of courtship.'

This sounded pompous – and also less than the truth. Women whom he found attractive tended to daunt him utterly so that he would never dare approach them.

Tilarwa continued to study him with her almond eyes. At times she seemed just like a child, at others – as now – very much the young woman approaching the prime of her urchin beauty.

'I must go,' she said abruptly, and she hurried out of the cubicle before Ethoam could say another word.

Vendavo stood under the central dome of the High Temple, drenched in the light which streamed through the Star Window. The faceted panes fractured the radiance into rainbow hues which splattered the white marble floor like multi-coloured rain.

It was still early and the temple was not yet open to the public; but he had had no difficulty in gaining admission and being left alone so that he could pursue his calling. The Star Window had been created centuries before by an unknown artist whose work adorned many temples throughout the land. In those days, artists were thoroughly pious and utterly convinced that their gifts were directly inspired by the Supreme Spirit. The priesthood embraced them wholeheartedly, certain that the chimeras were not only supernatural but holy.

Vendavo climbed the altar steps, drinking in the cool solemnity of the place, the soaring curved spaces, the dark recesses in which multitudes of candles glittered. Chimeras flocked around him with a fury of whispers as he studied the figures and bas-reliefs of those who had preceded him. Above the altar, mounted on a pedestal, was the statue of the first woman Hierarch, an artist herself who had reputedly founded the religion of the land and raised the first temples after proclaiming the chimeras the Heavenly Host, the spirits of those who had departed the earth.

The life-sized statue was pitted and worn, but its major features were still well-defined. It had been discovered half-buried in the garden of an abattoir razed to make way for the new road to Jormalu's bridge. It was popularly believed to be a self-portrait, a chimera wrought by the Hierarch herself, gaily coloured and lifelike when first fashioned.

Vendavo had never been a great frequenter of temples, and this was the first time he had studied the figure in any detail. By today's standards its execution was crude, and he found himself annoyed by the incongruously noble features, the air of serene gravity. The Hierarch had lived at a time when a ruler needed to be decisive and ruthless, and he had a vision of a domineering and fiery woman with the face of a termagant; nobility and serenity had no place in it. The statue could not possibly represent the real woman of history.

He descended the steps, satisfied that he would derive no inspiration from the works of other artists. He always gave of his best when he clung to the purity of his own vision and allowed nothing to dilute it.

In Temple Park, pedlars, beggars and lovers sat under the shade of flowering jacarandas, while street artists performed to small knots of people, just as he had done many years before. He hurried on, aware that he had spent longer in the temple than he had imagined; morning was well advanced.

On a cobbled lane, he entered a herbalist's; Nyssa had asked him to fetch an ointment for their new daughter's fever. The smells of camphor, aniseed and aromatic oils filled his nostrils. A woman sat at a table.

He passed her the slip of paper on which the doctor had written the ingredients for the ointment. As she studied it, she said, 'You're the artist, aren't you? Vendavo. I've seen you perform.'

She had hooded eyes, a chipped tooth at the front of her mouth, a tousled look. The top of her blouse was loosely tied, revealing the half-globe of a breast.

'I can sense your creatures,' she said.

He eyed her. Cautiously he asked, 'Do you create yourself?'

She shook her head, utterly dismissing the idea. Her response pleased him; he was constantly being pestered by those who claimed to be 'sensitive' and wanted him to tell them the secret of how to fashion chimeras. The secret, he always replied, was to begin.

'Can the ointment be prepared immediately?' he asked.

'Of course.'

She retreated through a beaded curtain into a tiny room crammed with bottles, phials and jars. The curtain had a gap in it, and he watched her mixing the ointment in a mortar bowl, her every movement languid yet assured. She was a woman thoroughly at ease with herself, and there was no denying her rough handsomeness. Presently she emerged with a small glass jar which she laid on the counter.

He put a hand into his purse, but she shook her head.

'Create something for me.'

He smiled, and instantly a vision came to mind and a chimera rippled through him.

On the counter formed a miniature of the woman, the likeness at once flattering yet true. She lay on her back, naked, her arms outstretched as if awaiting the embrace of a lover.

Vendavo returned her smile.

'Are you alone here?' he asked.

She laughed.

Tilarwa entered the cubicle and surprised Ethoam by immediately kneeling on the cushion. Normally she did not visit him so frequently, and he had not noticed her in the temple when he had arrived earlier.

'What's happened to your hair?' he asked. It had been severely and crudely cut so that it now hung ragged about her ears.

'I did it myself.'

In her hands she held something wrapped in muslin. Head bowed, she thrust it at him.

'What is it?' he asked.

'A cake. I baked it for you.'

He opened it up. It was heavy and dark, redolent of treacle and vine fruits.

'I know you like cakes,' she said. 'I saw you on the street yesterday morning, buying sugared pastries at a stall.'

Ethoam knew she lived close by, but he had the uncomfortable feeling that she had been spying on him. In fact, he had bought the pastries for a blind veteran of Andrak's wars who was presently dying in one of the Comforters' retreats; all that was left to him was his sweet tooth. Ethoam was dismayed at the idea that Tilarwa would assume his corpulence was due to over-indulgence; for years he had eaten like a sparrow, but his belly had not diminished one whit. Nevertheless, he was touched by the gift.

'It's very kind of you.'

'I burnt the first one I made. My father says I'm good for nothing.'

She spoke without self-pity, but her head remained bowed. Only now did Ethoam notice the graze on her chin. Gingerly, he reached down and put his hand under her jawbone.

'Did your father do that?' he asked.

She said nothing.

'Did he?'

'He has a new husband for me. A merchant who trades in cloth.'

Ethoam leaned forward, making a show of examining her face.

'Have you met him?'

'I cut my hair so I would look terrible. He has foul breath and the manners of a pig. I hate him more than the undertaker.'

'And no doubt you told your father as much.'

88

'I told him I intended to marry someone else.'

'Indeed? And is that true?'

'Yes.' There was a pause, and then she looked up at him. 'Can you guess who it might be?'

Ethoam was genuinely perplexed, and only when he saw the look of irritation in her face did realization dawn.

'I've told my father you'll visit us tomorrow evening.'

Ethoam was speechless.

'You must help me. He'll send the merchant packing if you do.'

Already she was on her feet. She gave him directions to her house, told him what time he was expected, then departed as suddenly as she had come.

Ethoam did not attempt to pursue her. He simply sat there for long moments afterwards, quite stunned, quite unable to decide whether she had been serious or not. No, it was impossible. Tilarwa was young and spirited, and it was simply ludicrous that she would want to spend the rest of her life with a fat and bumbling servant of the temple such as himself, even as a pretext to avoid marriage to the merchant.

The curtain opened and Nisbisi peeped into the cubicle. She frowned – her face seemed perfectly formed for it – and said, 'Have you finished your duties?'

'Indeed.'

'Isn't there other work for you to do on the streets?'

She disliked him lingering in the temple. In general the priesthood tolerated rather than welcomed Comforters, often deeming them insufficiently holy since they were not fully consecrated and spent much of their time in what were considered to be secular pursuits.

'I was thinking,' Ethoam told her. 'Meditating.'

'What's that?' she said. 'A cake?'

He was still holding it in his hands. 'It looks remarkably like one.'

'A gift from the girl?'

He thrust it at her, knowing he was obliged to hand over all offerings to the temple. No doubt she would scoff the lot at supper with her novices.

'That girl is becoming a frequent visitor,' she remarked. 'Is it wise to encourage her?'

'I'm surprised you noticed. Do you keep track of all my petitioners?'

It was unlike him to be so sharp, and he immediately felt abashed. Under her withering stare, he slipped past her and hurried out of the temple.

The streets were filled with evening shadows. Ethoam pushed all thoughts of Tilarwa from his mind, climbing a rutted track towards the old quarter of the city. He followed a circuitous route to the house, checking along the way to ensure he was not being followed. Such precautions made him feel foolish, but they were necessary.

Insaan the tailor had rooms above a disused warehouse in a secluded backstreet. The eight others were already present when Ethoam arrived – punctuality had never been his strong point – along with Melicort, one of the personal assistants to Alkanere, the leader that none of them had ever met.

'Have you heard the news?' Insaan said immediately, and with great excitement. 'The uprising will begin on the day the bridge is opened!'

Ethoam stood there, slack-mouthed, while the others hugged him and slapped his back. Unlike most of them, he was a relative newcomer to the group, having joined it only three years before. At their meetings, they constantly talked of overthrowing Jormalu and his government, but it was hard to believe that the uprising was actually now at hand.

Melicort was already preparing to leave, having other groups to address before sunset. A short, red-headed man, he had the intense eyes and brisk movements which Ethoam had observed in other deeply committed reformers; it was as if he couldn't wait to bring about the new order which he was always promising was at hand.

'You'll receive fuller instructions on the day,' he told them. But everyone pleaded for more details, and he paused at the door.

'There's going to be an entertainment on the bridge to mark its opening. The artist Vendavo is performing a pageant of some description. That's when we'll strike.'

And then he was gone, Insaan shepherding him out. Ethoam stared after him, stunned by the mention of Vendavo's name.

*　　　*　　　*

Perched on a low stool, Vendavo let the ghostly figures swim in the air while the chimeras seethed about him. He wore only a loose shirt and leggings, and he was soaked with sweat. Since dawn he had been summoning up figures of every shape and variety, examining and rejecting them, taking a feature here, a mannerism there, then combining them into something new, a phantom with the striking characteristics he needed. All the while he had to hold the chimeras at bay, resisting their urge to be made fully real. The preparation of the image, straining the imagination to conjure up all the details and idiosyncrasies that would make it vivid and memorable, was always the hardest part, like mining gold from thin air. Once done, bringing it to life was child's play.

At present he was working on Jormalu's great-grandfather, who had separated the Hierarchy from the temples by declaring himself a secular ruler and the chimeras natural creatures of the air, unconnected with the Supreme Spirit. By doing so, he had strengthened his own power while freeing artists from the constraints of piety. Traditionally he was portrayed as an ascetic and an intellectual, but he was also known to have been fond of oratory and of the sport of wrestling, in which he often participated himself. Considering this, Vendavo suddenly found his representation of a lean and cadaverous figure in white robes utterly inadequate and inapt.

With a fury of exasperation, he dissolved everything. Around him the chimeras recoiled and retreated, their hectic inarticulate babble fading to a murmur. Vendavo let out a great sigh, clearing both his lungs and his head.

Slowly the chimeras began to flitter back into his vicinity, their manner hesitant, querulous. Already he had begun to revise his image. Yesterday, in the park, he had seen a burly beggar accosting passersby, vehemently demanding coins. With robes instead of rags, a sceptre in place of a walking stick, rings on manicured fingers, the beggar could be transformed –

'I hope you'll excuse the intrusion.'

Vendavo spun around. Mersulis was standing there, as black as a shadow. He had not even heard the stable door open.

'I hope you don't mind me visiting,' she said. 'I simply wondered how you were progressing.'

Normally nothing could distract him when he was working;

he could create anywhere. But this was a particularly difficult and ambitious undertaking, and Mersulis had disturbed him at a crucial moment.

He summoned up his new vision of Jormalu's great-grandfather, sending it racing towards Mersulis, its arms outstretched menacingly.

To her credit, Mersulis did not scream, though her surprise and alarm were evident. She simply took a step back, far too late to prevent the hands from closing around her throat . . .

But of course they passed harmlessly through her, as insubstantial as the figure itself. Even if he had made it fully solid, it could not have harmed her. There was something about chimeras which made them shy from human contact during their summoning. They could never be made to actively injure living things.

Vendavo allowed the figure to dissolve away while Mersulis recovered her composure. At length she said, 'Who was it?'

He told her.

'Ah,' she said. 'Interesting. I'd always imagined him differently.'

'We each have our own image of things.'

She ran a finger under the collar of her tunic. A mist of sweat had formed on her face and neck.

'Are you basing your work on the Chronicles?' she asked.

He nodded. 'They're the only source we have.'

'But there's very little physical description in them.'

'To my mind, that's a freedom rather than a restriction. One has, inevitably, to interpret. I've assumed that I would be allowed complete freedom in this respect.'

'Oh, perfect freedom, have no fears on that score. But you won't forget that Jormalu will want to see . . .' she hesitated, choosing her words, '. . . a progression of nobility and achievement up to our own time.'

'Of course. The display will emphasize that.'

Mersulis leaned against a stall-post, undoing the top button of her tunic. She was much taller than most Southerners, and in certain lights her skin looked like black suede. She radiated an utter confidence in both her status and her beauty.

'How do you credit the Chronicles?' she asked.

Vendavo eyed her. By all accounts, Jormalu trusted her

implicitly and frequently took her advice on matters of state. She had lasted far longer than his two previous wives, and his affection for her was apparently undiminished.

'In what sense?' he said.

'In the sense in which we read them. As history.'

Vendavo affected to consider. 'I'm no historian. They certainly tell a vivid story.'

'Of that there's no doubt. Today's historians will tell you that their chronology is doubtful and their genealogies certainly spurious. But they will only say so in private.'

She was smiling, as though challenging him to comment. Of course he knew that the Chronicles, written by a variety of hands over the course of several hundred years, often reported events decades or centuries after they had happened and usually presented them in a manner designed to flatter the ruler of the day.

'I'm no expert on these matters,' he said. 'I read the words and bring my imagination to bear.'

Mersulis nodded, still smiling. 'And so do we all. We each create history in our own image, wouldn't you say?'

It was such a smile: teasing, enigmatic, nothing whatever to do with humour or good-will.

Ethoam sat opposite Tilarwa at the dinner table, telling her of his strained relationship with Nisbisi and his belief that the priesthood was in general idle and self-satisfied, their attitude towards Comforters high-handed. True, he was not as devoted in a religious sense as someone like Nisbisi was – in fact, if he was honest with himself, he had long ceased to believe that there really was a Supreme Spirit directing their destinies, irrespective of the existence of the chimeras. He was an agent of the temple who counselled prayer without faith in its usefulness, an apostate who only continued to practise his calling for the practical good it did.

Throughout all this, Tilarwa listened while clearing dishes, pouring more wine and serving fried bananas in a creamy sauce. Ethoam felt positively indulged, the meal far finer than any he had eaten in a long time; surely it spoke of her affection for him to have gone to such trouble.

She wore a lilac dress that was obviously her best. Between

them on the table was a small urn containing the widow Bila's ashes which he had given her on his arrival. Earlier he had officiated at Bila's cremation, and there were no relatives present to receive her earthly remains. The gift of a departed spirit's ashes was considered by many to be the profoundest token of esteem and affection.

Before arriving, he had imagined Tilarwa's house as a cramped hovel in some dingy alley, or a cluttered room in a tenement, the stairs rank with rotting food and dogs' droppings. He had spent his own childhood in such a tenement, though he and his brothers and sisters played outside in the street whenever they could, escaping both the fetid atmosphere and the squabbling of their shrewish mother and drunken father. It pained him to think so uncharitably of his parents, but they had never shown him any guidance or love, and he, the youngest, had been forced to rely on his elder brothers until a priest, assuming his timidness was something holy, had taken him into the temple at the age of ten. Only then had his education begun.

Tilarwa's house turned out to be a small but sturdy building at the corner of a street down which Ethoam had passed many times. Her father was not present, having gone to visit a cousin because, Tilarwa said, he was ashamed to meet his daughter's spiritual counsellor. This development unduly flustered Ethoam at first, and he tried to leave. But Tilarwa had cooked plantains and sweet potatoes with scraps of pork bought with money filched from a hoard her father kept hidden. There was also home-made apricot wine, which Ethoam began drinking freely to embolden himself. He now informed Tilarwa that Comforters were encouraged to marry since a settled family life was deemed to improve their ability to minister to others. He talked of his desire to have children, something which had never crossed his mind until now.

The wine was making him garrulous and indiscreet, but for some reason he did not want to stop talking; he wanted Tilarwa to know how he felt about such things so that, he reasoned, she would understand just what sort of man she intended to marry – if, indeed, she did intend it. A detached part of himself was aware that he was being foolish, undignified, possibly blasphemous. But the world and all its considerations had faded into the background; all that mattered, all he was aware of, was the dinner table and Tilarwa sitting opposite in her lilac dress. He might have talked all night had she not finally whispered, 'Hush.'

He stopped. She was smiling at him, the way an indulgent mother might smile at the excesses of a precocious child. Only then did he actually wonder how long he had been talking, and how much of what he had said was of any interest to her at all. With a crushing sense of embarrassment, he felt as if he had overstayed his welcome, strained her hospitality to breaking point, ruined the whole evening.

'Forgive me,' he spluttered. 'I didn't mean . . . I should leave now.'

He lurched up from his chair. The room slewed, and he would have fallen had not Tilarwa reached across the table to steady his arm.

He blubbered more apologies as she led him across to the armchair beside the hearth and ordered him to sit down.

'I must go,' he insisted. 'I must.'

She pointed to the window: the sky beyond was a deep blue.

'It's past sunset. You'll have to stay here.'

'No. I can't . . . Your father . . .'

'He won't be back tonight. No one need know. You can't go home like that.'

'I must.'

Then he began to hiccup. Bile rose in his throat. He swallowed air, held it down for as long as he could, exhaled it in a great blast. Miraculously, the hiccups ceased. He felt a great weariness, but became aware that Tilarwa was laughing at him. Then she was hauling him up from the armchair, leading him towards the stairs, telling him firmly she intended to put him to bed.

Again he protested that he preferred to risk the curfew than compromise her. Again she laughed and thrust him towards the stairs.

It was an arduous, humiliating business, with him panting and grunting like a sow. Finally they crawled into the attic room. Tilarwa pushed him on to a mattress covered with a worn patchwork quilt. She wrenched off his sandals. Then he felt her tugging at his robes.

'No,' he murmured, striving to sit upright, to force her hands away. The feather pillows suddenly set off a violent bout of sneezing. He found his handkerchief, blew his nose copiously. He felt ridiculous.

Again Tilarwa seemed to be laughing at him.

'Were you serious,' he said, 'about wanting to marry me?'

'It's hardly a joking matter, is it?'

'I've got nothing to offer you. Not even pleasing looks.'

She made a scoffing sound. 'Who are you to judge what I see in you? You're a good man – you have a good heart. When you spoke of how you hated the way the poor are treated, of how you want to fight for a better life for them – well, I feel the same. I'd like to be part of that fight.'

Suddenly she seemed so composed and adult. His memory of the evening was already hazy, but he had no recollection of saying any such thing.

'I'm just a Comforter. I do what I can.'

'Oh no,' she replied. 'I think you're much more than that. Let me help you, Ethoam. You can trust me.'

Another sneeze overtook him. He heaved himself off the bed, snatched up his sandals and began stumbling down the stairs. He heard her calling after him, but he was determined to brave the streets. Barefooted, he hurried to the door, wrenched it open, and fled into the night.

Their daughter had cried throughout the night, and the doctor had arrived early that morning and promptly announced that the crisis was coming. Vendavo sat in the anteroom with his five older children and their governess, listening to the child's whimpering, to Nyssa's exhausted words of comfort, to the physician's utter silence. He had little faith in doctors, for Nyssa herself had almost been killed by one when carrying Leshtu, their eldest. He was now a strapping boy of fifteen who sat, restless and bored, watching his younger brothers and sisters play with the miniature landscape and soldiers which Vendavo had created for them.

Sunshine poured into the room like something liquid and sweet. The day was well advanced, and Vendavo found it increasingly difficult to suppress his frustration. He wanted it to be over, one way or another. Their daughter was only a month old, and she had been sickly since birth. Because of this, they had not named her, for it was easier to lose a child that had no name. Of course he hoped she would survive, but he could not countenance many more broken nights or precious hours away from his work. Even now, the chimeras pestered him with their silvery babbling, despite all his efforts to banish them.

Not for the first time, the children began squabbling over the possession of a soldier. The governess tried to intervene, but her shrill voice only added to the noise. She was a thin-faced woman who wore sack-like dresses and stank of liniment. Vendavo's patience was exhausted.

'Enough!' he shouted. 'Take them outside.'

There was no protest, and the governess was soon bustling the children through the door. Only Shubi, his eldest daughter, lingered.

'Can I stay, Father?' she asked in her quiet voice. 'I won't be a nuisance.'

She was a blonde nine-year-old, a reflective, self-contained child with Nyssa's warm brown eyes. Vendavo had to admit she was his favourite, and he was seldom able to refuse her anything.

'Go and sit by the window,' he said.

With the others gone and the room reduced to silence, Vendavo became aware that in Nyssa's bedroom all was quiet too. Was their daughter finally asleep? Or had she given up the struggle to cling to life? He rose, intending to open the door and go in. But he did not take a step forward. Better to leave them alone. Better to wait. Sooner or later he would know, for good or ill.

He paced the room in slow strides, wanting the solitude of the stable and the imperatives of his vision. Again the chimeras thickened about him as he began contemplating his pageant. Though often irritated by their ceaseless, wordless demands, he did not feel truly alive without them.

'Father!'

Shubi spoke in an urgent whisper. She was sitting on the window-ledge, peering down into the street.

'Father!' she said again. 'Look!'

He crossed to the window. Three soldiers were dragging a young man into a narrow alleyway opposite the house. The man was fighting with them, flailing and kicking in their grasp, until one of the three elbowed him hard in the stomach. As he slumped, they dragged him deeper into the alley and flung him into a tangle of weeds. Clouds of dandelion seed rose as they kicked him about the body and head.

Finally the man lay still. One of the soldiers withdrew his sword and placed the tip on the man's abdomen. Leaning on the hilt, he drove it under the ribcage. The body spasmed, then went still. The soldier withdrew his sword and wiped the blade on the dead man's leggings before he and his two companions returned to the street and resumed their patrol.

Vendavo swept Shubi up in his arms, taking her away from the window.

'Why did they –' she began, but he put a finger to her lips. Staring hard into her serious eyes, he smiled.

'I did it. It was just a creation.'

She looked back at him. Plainly she did not believe him.

'Is the baby going to die?' she said.

'Let's hope not,' he said. 'Shall I conjure something else for you?'

'I want to go and see.'

'No,' he said firmly, unsure of what exactly she meant. 'We have to wait here. Be patient.'

But at that moment the bedroom door opened and the doctor stepped out.

Ethoam lingered on the corner of the street, filled with indecision. Above him, pigeons were roosting in the eaves of a house, their cooing like a conspiracy in code.

Evening had lengthened the shadows, but dusk would not fall for some time yet. He watched a woman putting a dish of rice in a small street shrine. Everything continued as normal, yet it was far from normal. He had gone about his duties as usual, uttering his vain litanies of comfort to the sick and the helpless, but his mind was entirely elsewhere. And so he finished his work early and took a barge across the river. The house fronted the waterside, and the windows which faced the street were small and narrow, giving it a slightly forbidding aspect.

Still he did not move, still he was uncertain of what to do.

It was all a question of trust, that most unreliable of human virtues.

A group of soldiers entered the street and began to walk in his direction. This hastened his decision. He strode across to the door and tugged on the bell-pull.

The woman who answered was the stern-featured governess; Ethoam could not remember her name. She did not recognize him instantly, which did not surprise him; over two years had passed since his last visit.

'I'm here to see Vendavo,' he announced.

It was only then that recognition seemed to dawn in her face. She gave a curt bow of the head. 'Of course. Come in.'

Inside, it was cool, the evening sunlight mellowing the austere white walls and marble of the reception hall. She led him through into the main room, where Nyssa sat with a baby cradled in her arms while the rest of the children played at her feet. On seeing him, she smiled and said his name.

She rose, still holding the baby, came across and kissed him on the cheek.

'Another one?' he said, peering at the sleeping child.

Nyssa nodded. 'A daughter. You came at a good time, because she needs a blessing. She's only just recovered from a fever which almost killed her.'

Nyssa looked haggard, her eyes sunk in grey hollows, her hair lank and tousled. The children were watching him, and he realized he had never seen the youngest boy before.

'It's been too long since you last visited us,' Nyssa was saying to him. 'Have you been keeping well?'

'Well enough,' he said, studying the children. 'They've all grown.'

'Time slips by.'

'Is Vendavo here?'

'He's taking a nap. I'll wake him.'

'There's no need. I can wait.'

'Nonsense. He'll be pleased to see you.'

She went through into the study, leaving Ethoam to the attentions of the children.

'You're Uncle Ethoam, aren't you?' said one of the girls.

'I'm pleased you remember me.'

'The last time you came you brought us toffee.'

'You *do* have a good memory. I'm sorry to say I've got nothing for you today.'

'You can name the baby. None of us can decide.'

There was a hearty cry of 'Biru!' and Vendavo appeared, striding over and embracing Ethoam warmly.

Only Vendavo called him by his old name, but he did not object since he often thought of his brother as Neni; his fame as an artist belonged indeed to Vendavo, who was somehow another person from the elder brother who had taught him how to steal melons from market stalls, how to shin up walls, catch moths with candles and glass jars, the brother who had shepherded him through the hazardous streets of their youth and entertained him with gaudy displays of his talent.

Ethoam noted that his brother was thicker around the waist and wore his hair longer than before. He was unshaven and looked dishevelled with sleep. But he still had his good looks, his ease of manner, his powerful physical presence.

'Did you come to see our newest one?' he asked.

'That was fortunate,' Ethoam admitted. 'She's as lovely as her mother. It's as well you can support your ever-growing brood.'

Ethoam spoke good-naturedly. He did not envy Vendavo, despite his gifts, and never advertised the fact that he was his younger brother. Not even Nisbisi knew. If anything, he had sought more anonymity as his brother's fame grew. Their lives were very different, and it was not always easy to approve of his activities; but there was a blood bond to be honoured, past loyalties to be repaid.

'So,' Vendavo said, 'what brings you here today, if it's not simply good fortune?'

'A matter of some importance.' Ethoam turned to Nyssa. 'Would you mind if we spoke alone?'

'Come through into the study,' he said, taking Ethoam by the arm.

The study was a big room whose wide balcony overlooked the river. A sofa and several floorcushions were the only furniture apart from crude wooden shelves on which stood an infinite variety of small stone chimeras – figures, animals, flowers, trees, houses, even miniature landscapes.

Ethoam paused at the centre of the study, trying to sense the presence of unformed chimeras. But he could hear nothing, feel nothing. It had always been that way, even when they were small boys and Neni used to tell him of how the chimeras assailed his mind, of their ceaseless urge to be shaped. He was deaf and insensate to them.

From a shelf Vendavo produced a bottle of wine and two cups.

'Refreshment for honoured guests,' he said, and led Ethoam out on to the balcony.

They sat down on recliners. Red wine sloshed into the cups. Ethoam watched his brother, feeling a strong sense of both kinship and estrangement. They were the only two of seven children who had escaped the poverty and disease of the streets. The rest of the family – their parents and all their brothers and sisters – had succumbed to sickness and neglect while he was still a young apprentice at the temple.

Ethoam essayed only a small sip of wine before setting his cup down on the floor. The sun burnished the river and lit the pale blue triangular sail of a fishing boat that was returning from the sea. Smoke rose from chimneys as ovens were stoked for evening meals.

'Well, Biru,' Vendavo said, 'what's this matter you wish to discuss?'

'A matter of violence in Veridi-Almar.'

Vendavo turned his head to face him.

'Before I say any more, I must have your promise as a brother that you'll say nothing of what I'm going to tell you to anyone else. Not even Nyssa.'

'It sounds like a serious business.'

'It is. And you're involved in it, whether you like it or not.'

Now the blue eyes were filled with an avid curiosity. 'Involved? Involved in what?'

'First I must have your promise that you'll say nothing to anyone.'

'I promise. What have I to do with this business, Biru?'

Ethoam could hear the sailors on the fishing boat calling to one another. At that moment he became convinced he was making a grave mistake. But it was too late to stop now.

'There's going to be an uprising on the day the bridge is opened. We aim to overthrow Jormalu.'

101

Vendavo was silent for a moment. He raised his cup to his lips.

'We?'

'I'm one of those who oppose the Hierarchy.'

'You?' Vendavo sat up, genuinely surprised. 'You, Biru? For how long?'

'For some time.'

'But why?'

'Because I want to see justice for all our people.'

'You amaze me. I never thought – well, you hardly seem the firebrand.'

'I believe we have a duty to those less fortunate than ourselves.'

He could see his brother beginning to think furiously. He had always been quick-witted, rescuing Ethoam on many occasions from the attentions of bullies or irate stallholders with smooth words or startling chimeras. Memories came to him of white mice, voluptuous nudes, sudden snow flurries, a scattering of silver coins. But that was long ago.

'Do you want a donation for your cause?' Vendavo asked. 'Is that why you're here?'

'There will be a rising on the day the bridge is opened,' Ethoam repeated. 'I'm not here for money.'

'Then I can't see why this should concern me.'

'We know you're planning some display for the Hierarch's benefit. You'll be caught in the middle of the fighting.'

Now there was a long silence. Below them, the twilit river slid past, heavy, unstoppable. At night, Jormalu's soldiers dumped the bodies of his enemies into its waters. Most of them were cast back up on its muddy banks long before reaching the sea, their eyes pecked out by gulls, their limbs gnawed by rats.

'If you tell anyone about this,' Ethoam said, 'then I and perhaps hundreds of others may die before –'

'I'm well aware of that!' Vendavo snapped. He stood up, began pacing the balcony. 'The question is – why have you told me, and what am I supposed to do about it?'

Ethoam knew he was angry because now he had been placed in a dilemma, something he disliked unless it was a practical matter of his art.

'I've told you because I'm your brother and I want you to save yourself. I don't want to see Nyssa a widow and your children fatherless.'

Vendavo was gripping the balcony rail with both hands. Lights had begun to shine in the houses on the north bank as twilight deepened. Without turning, he said, 'What am I to do?'

'There's only one thing to do. You must find a pretext to cancel the performance.'

A veil of cloud coated the sky, and lightning flickered within it. The sun was like a gold coin drowned under milky water. There was no rain, and the air was still, as thick as syrup.

Vendavo sat with Mersulis and Jormalu's two young children in a palace courtyard, watching striped fish drift through the dull water of an ornamental pool. Dragonflies hovered over magnolia waterlilies, snapping up the insects that darted on the surface of the water.

Mersulis waved a black lace fan in front of her face while Vendavo watched the two children play with the fanciful galleons he had created, tentatively launching them from the edge of the pool. The boy was twelve, the girl ten, both offspring of the Hierarch's second wife. They were silent and serious-faced children, their manners impeccable.

'Sometimes he has unexpected visitors wait all day,' Mersulis remarked. 'Sometimes they have to wait even longer. You should have told me you wanted an audience with him.'

'It was a sudden decision.'

'I hope it's nothing too serious. Nothing that will affect your performance tomorrow.'

Vendavo made a noncommittal sound. Mersulis had been pressing him to tell her the reason for his visit ever since he had arrived at the palace, but he was determined to say nothing until he was in Jormalu's presence.

Thunder growled in the distance, and a thin heat-haze blurred the exotic trees and shrubbery of the chimera-garden which Vendavo had created for the Hierarch years before. Everything seemed utterly motionless, any sound swiftly swallowed up by the heavy air.

The fan moved silently in Mersulis's hand. She wore a

tight-fitting sheathed gown of black silk which left her shoulders bare. It flared below the knees, revealing her slim yet muscular legs. Black slippers were loosely strapped to her ankles.

'It's the rainy season in the south,' she observed. 'When I was a child, I used to sail boats made of bark down the main street of our village during the flood.'

'You were born in a village?'

'We lived there for part of the summer. It was quite large. My father always liked the jungle.' She kicked off a slipper and stretched out her leg to dip her toes in the water of the pool. 'Did you know I was responsible for his death?'

Her father had been the ruler of the southern peoples until the armies of Jormalu's father had subjugated them. Later he had been installed as a puppet governor before an attempted rebellion during the early years of Jormalu's reign led to his execution. Mersulis's survival – and her present status – were all the more remarkable as a result.

'I always hated him,' she said in the same conversational tone as before. 'He had many nasty habits, especially his determination to take me into his bed as soon as I was old enough. Shall I tell you how I revenged myself on him?'

Vendavo watched the ripples spread from her foot. She wanted no reply.

'You may recall that several years ago the province was restive. Chiefly it was due to my father's poor governorship and the corruption of officials who worked under him. He was negligent and lazy rather than corrupt himself, but the unrest became so serious that Jormalu himself came south at the head of an army.'

She paused, and glanced across at the children. They were out of earshot.

'Jormalu had tired of his wife, and was already planning to have her executed. I saw my opportunity. I made myself fully available to him, offering not only the kind of comforts which all men desire from women but also good counsel. There was serious danger of a full-scale revolt which would require considerable force to suppress. By taking my advice, Jormalu was able to avoid any great bloodshed. He denounced my father as the source of the people's troubles, had him publicly executed and promised immediate reforms. Then, with his wife disposed

104

of, he married me as a gesture of his good-will and affection towards the province.'

The boats had begun to bobble in the water as Mersulis created waves with her foot. Vendavo did not dare look at her.

'Don't misunderstand me,' she said. 'I acted expediently because I knew it would benefit not only myself but also the people of my province. *Anything* is better than death.'

He wondered what she was trying to tell him. Jormalu's promised reforms in the south had never been implemented, and the province was once more restive.

On the pool, both boats capsized. Within moments they had sunk. The children watched the bubbling water, showing neither alarm nor disappointment but simply a grave scrutiny.

'Give them new ones,' Mersulis whispered to him.

As always, he was attended by chimeras, and it was a simple matter to do as he was ordered. He conjured a pair of galleons even finer than before, placing them on the water where their predecessors had sunk. Only the briefest of glances at Vendavo betrayed the children's pleasure.

'Take them out of the water,' Mersulis called to them. 'Then you can go inside.'

The children obeyed, hurrying off through one of the arched entranceways.

'They're well behaved,' Vendavo said. 'Mine squabble like crows.'

'They were made aware from an early age of the need for dignity. Jormalu is a strict father.'

'You seem to have a good bond with them.'

'Considering that I was instrumental in the death of their mother, you mean?'

He stole a look at her. If anything, she appeared amused.

'I think we are alike, you and I,' she said. 'We do what is necessary in the circumstances while giving ourselves room for manoeuvre. I think we understand one another perfectly.'

He had begun to wonder why she had spoken so freely about herself. The answer became strikingly obvious as she continued to gaze at him with candid eyes. She was binding him to her, making sure he owned a secret whose selling-price would be his death, because she desired him. And though he understood the dangers, he was also aroused. Chimeras thickened invisibly around him as he imagined Mersulis submitting to him in some private chamber, a black amazon on a battleground of white sheets, a formidable and demanding lover who would test his mettle.

At that moment, one of the household guard appeared, marching briskly forward.

'The Hierarch will see you now.'

Accompanied by Mersulis, Vendavo was led along a labyrinth of marbled corridors to another courtyard where Jormalu, a dumpy figure in purple robes, stood stroking the flank of a white horse while a retainer held its reins.

Middle-age had made the Hierarch look bloated, but there was still a youthfulness, almost an adolescence, about his features. In recent years he had developed a passion for horse-racing and was having the palace gardens modified so that a track could be made through them.

'Well?' he said, his back to Vendavo. 'How does your work progress?'

Vendavo hesitated before saying, 'It progresses well, my lord.'

'Then what are you doing here?'

The Hierarch spoke with patent irritation. Once more, Mersulis looked amused, and only then did Vendavo appreciate the full extent of her ruthlessness.

'I have something to tell you,' he said.

Ethoam was shaving by candlelight when he heard the knock on the door. He froze, staring at his startled face in the mirror. Dawn had not yet broken, and he was expecting no visitors.

He snuffed out the candle. The knock came again. Creeping over to the window, he peeked out through a gap in the shutter. He could see nothing.

His house was a small single-roomed stone building with only one door. There was nowhere for him to hide. For the past few days he had dreaded that the soldiers would come. He was not a brave man, and he knew only too well that he would be tortured if he was arrested. And the arrest itself would be a likely sign that the uprising had failed even before it had begun.

Again the knock. But it was not brutal and peremptory,

106

the heavy hand of the military, but urgent and impatient, a brisk rapping. Still he waited, hoping that he might succeed in persuading his caller that the house was empty.

'Ethoam!' came a voice. 'I know you're there.'

He pulled the bolts on the door, swung it open. Tilarwa stood alone on his doorstep.

'What are you doing on the streets at this hour?' he said to her. 'You'll be arrested.'

'All the more reason for letting me in.'

He did not want to court the attention of any dawn patrols, so he ushered her inside and closed the door. Then he had to fumble in the dark for a match to relight the candle.

The room filled with a shadowy yellow light.

'One of the novices at the temple told me where you lived,' Tilarwa said. 'You haven't been to your cubicle in days.'

'I've had other things to attend to.'

Unexpectedly, her face broke into a grin. Ethoam realized that he was standing there in his undershirt, his face patched with shaving soap. He went back to the basin and put a towel to his cheeks before reaching for his robes.

'Why are you here?' he said. 'What do you want?'

'I want to help.'

'Help? Help in what?'

'You know what. The rising. I want to be a part of it.'

He began to search the floor for his sandals. 'I know nothing about that.'

'The city's filled with rumours. It's today, isn't it?'

He tugged hard on his buckles. 'I've told you I know nothing about that.'

'You think I'm stupid, don't you? A stupid girl.'

'Oh no,' he said softly. 'Not at all.'

'Then let me help.' She came forward, touched his arm.

Birds had begun to sing in the fields which bordered his house. He threw open a window. The sky was lightening, and the air was heavy with the promise of a storm.

'Let me help,' Tilarwa said again. 'Let me be at your side when the fighting starts. That's all I ask.'

He wanted so much to believe her. 'I have duties I must attend to this morning. Alone.'

'Then tell me where I can meet you later.'

107

She looked so pretty in the candlelight, her eyes dark and wide. Sighing, he said, 'Very well . . .'

Soon after dawn, the storm finally broke. All morning the downpour continued unabated while thunder resonated over the city and lightning veined the livid clouds. In the streets, swelling streams of water began to carry the detritus of the city – rags, papers, rotting food, dead rats and ordure. Everyone huddled in their houses, with not even a soldier to be seen. The only sound was the hammering of the rain.

Towards noon, the storm ended as abruptly as it had begun, the cloud dissolving away as the sun burned through again. Soon it was as hot as before and there was little trace of the rain except for caked rivulets of mud in the gutters.

Soldiers were the first to emerge, some on horseback, others on foot, all heavily armed. They manned the corners of all the main thoroughfares and massed at both ends of the bridge. Vendavo watched from his window, the house utterly silent around him. He had sent Nyssa and the children to their home in the mountains – ostensibly for Nyssa and the baby to recuperate. Nyssa had wanted to stay and see his pageant, but he was adamant she leave. She had not pressed him to tell her what was wrong.

Silence. And stillness. There was scarcely a trace of a chimera, and never had he felt more alone, more at the mercy of imponderables. Already nobles and dignitaries had gathered on the bridge, arrayed in all their finery. Then the Hierarch's golden carriage, drawn by six white horses, made its stately progress to the centre while soldiers massed along the parapet walls. Now musicians, acrobats and mime artists were performing as a prelude to the climax of the opening ceremony – his pageant. Afterwards there was to be a great feast at the palace where he would be guest-of-honour.

His mouth was dry, his stomach knotted. Presently a troop of six soldiers came marching down the street. They stopped outside his front door. Then they knocked.

Vendavo did his best to compose himself. He had decided against wearing the new white tunic which had been tailored for the occasion, and was instead garbed in sober greys and browns which would make him less readily distinguishable in a crowd. He draped his cloak over one shoulder and opened the door.

Without a word, he accompanied the guards down the street towards the bridge. A scattering of commoners watched as he went by, some offering words of encouragement and good luck, others saying nothing at all. Overhead, the sun shone fierce in a limpid blue sky.

Near the bridge, the crowds were thicker. Footsoldiers were massed in ranks, keeping them at bay. A uniformed avenue opened up for him as he marched forward with his guard of honour. A few cheers went up, but not many. The crowd seemed subdued, as if expectant of something other than entertainment.

More soldiers stood at the prows of vessels which filled the waters of the Raimus on both sides of the bridge. Never had he seen so many boats – barges, sailing craft, sloops, trawlers, caravels. They rang bells normally used only in fog.

At its midpoint the bridge bulged outwards, and tiered steps descended from the heightened parapets. Here the rich and respectable were thronged – merchants, bankers, the priesthood and the lesser and greater lords. In the centre of the open space a single huge block of masonry was missing. Originally Jormalu had intended to end the opening ceremony by lowering the final slab of stone into the hole by means of a windlass; but at the last moment Vendavo had presented him with a far more palatable alternative.

He had gone to the palace intending to tell the Hierarch of the plot against him. But something about his conversation with Mersulis prior to his audience – he could not say what it was – made him decide otherwise. And so instead he asked Jormalu for permission to end his pageant with the most dramatic creation of all – a statue of Jormalu himself, astride a miniature version of the bridge, which he would then place as the final stone in the structure, a permanent memorial to its creator. As he had anticipated, Jormalu readily gave his approval to the scheme.

The Hierarch sat with Mersulis and his two children on a red velvet sofa under a tasselled awning. His green-uniformed household guard surrounded him. As he was led forward, Vendavo tried to concentrate his mind on the pageant he intended to create – a visual history of the Hierarchy from its beginnings to the present. He had laboured long and hard to make each chapter spectacular in every respect, but for the first time he could bring no images to mind. His head was empty and the chimeras had deserted him utterly. Despite the crowds and the noise, he was engulfed in silence and solitude.

Vendavo bowed before the Hierarch. Jormalu flicked a fly-whisk in front of his face; he looked hot, peevish. Mersulis, strikingly dressed for once in white, favoured him with one of her ambiguous smiles, while the two children sat with their hands folded in their laps, their faces composed in expressions of virtuous forbearance.

Jormalu eyed him without favour.

'Your audience awaits you,' he said. 'Are you ready?'

He had never been more unready, but he nodded. Jormalu rose and addressed the crowd: 'The artist Vendavo will now perform for us.'

Vendavo turned, all eyes on him. The sun beat down, and he felt as if he was shrivelling under it, as if he might faint. The larger silence which now emanated from his audience, expectant and demanding, was the mirror-image of the blankness in his mind. He scanned the crowd, the soldiers, searching for the merest hint that the rebellion was about to begin. He looked for a sword slowly being drawn, a surreptitious signal between two men, the silent flight of an arrow, a movement on the waterfront. But there was nothing, and he could not keep his audience waiting any longer.

Panic began to well up in him. And then, just as he felt that he was going to be overwhelmed by it, as if he would never create again, a seething rush enveloped him, a host of babbling creatures demanding his attentions as the barbarian warlord sprang to life in his mind, a yellow-eyed savage on a foam-streaked horse, shouting oaths of triumph as he rode through the blazing city . . .

Ethoam stood at the rear of the crowd, trying to stop himself from sneezing as the fox-fur on the edges of Nisbisi's gown made his nostrils peppery.

He had to admit that Vendavo was not failing the crowd, producing tableau after tableau of startling force – images of

110

invaders razing cities, storming citadels, handing down laws, making treaties with other rulers, even giving bread to the poor in the depths of a snowy winter. The tableaux were taken from the Chronicles, but Vendavo had instilled his own special vision and power into them. In every scene the ordinary people featured in some way, not always as victims of great events but an appreciative audience to them, so that the message was ambiguous, a glorification of the Hierarchs but also an affirmation of the dignity and steadfastness of those who were ruled by them, an acknowledgement of their importance in the scheme of things.

It was clever, but then Vendavo had always been clever. Ethoam was surprised when he had discovered that the display was going ahead as planned, but then the day had been full of surprises. In the teeming rain he had hurried to Insaan's house to receive instructions on his part in the uprising, only to discover that Melicort had left orders that he was to return to the temple and conduct his duties as normal. The others in the group regarded him with a mixture of pity and suspicion, and he suddenly felt like an outcast, someone they no longer trusted. No explanation was offered for Melicort's decision, and he was not made privy to the plan of action for the day.

Rebuffed, he went to the temple as instructed and found Nisbisi full of high-minded anticipation. She had been invited to the opening ceremony, and it was she who confirmed that Vendavo was performing as planned. At this news, Ethoam was determined not to spend his day skulking in the temple or wandering the streets, so he announced that he was Vendavo's brother and begged her to let him accompany her to the ceremony. At first she would not believe him, so he fetched from his house a figurine which he normally kept locked in a chest. It was inscribed TO BIRU, WITH BROTHERLY LOVE, and the craftsmanship was unmistakable. Nisbisi knew that Biru was his old name, and he had gambled that she was enough of a snob to relish the prospect of having the artist's brother at her side during the opening ceremony, even if he was only a humble Comforter. And so it proved. Ethoam had spent much of the morning going through interminable introductions to eminent members of the priesthood while they waited for his brother to arrive.

111

Now Vendavo paced about, while the latest of his creations solidified close to the missing square of masonry at the centre of the arena. An almost complete circle of figures now surrounded the hole, all remarkably detailed and vividly coloured, monuments of genius to rulers wholly unworthy of them. No artist before his brother had ever had such control over his creations; no one could twist them so effortlessly into whatever shape he chose.

A chimera of Jormalu's father, Andrak, appeared. He was presiding over the trial of a peasant who, it was clear from a mime, had been accused of theft. Six men just like the accused sat under Andrak's pedestal, and it was they who consulted each other before one of them whispered into the Hierarch's ear. Andrak listened, then nodded, before emphatically motioning that the man was to be freed.

The watching Jormalu applauded, and the rest of the audience quickly joined in. Ethoam took the opportunity to blow his nose, reflecting that while Andrak had indeed introduced trial by jury, he had chiefly used it to eliminate all his rivals on trumped-up charges.

A hush fell once more as Andrak's chimera congealed into solidity. The circle was now complete. Ethoam kept glancing around. Ever since arriving on the bridge, he had been waiting for the fighting to break out, but there was no sign of it. The crowd remained orderly, and the guards lolled against the walls of the bridge, looking hot and bored.

At the centre of the circle, a chimera of Jormalu now shimmered into existence above a diminutive replica of the bridge. It was a convincing rendition, even if the figure was rather taller and less plump than in real life, its features more finely cast. As the crowd burst into applause, a fit of sneezing overtook Ethoam. In response to Nisbisi's furious stare – he had sprayed her in the process – Ethoam backed away up the steps, escaping the press of bodies.

On the river, the barges and boats had closed around the bridge. Rope-ladders were trailing down to them and men were frantically clambering up, actively assisted by the guards on the walls. It was a moment before Ethoam realized what was happening: the ferrymen had no love of the bridge and must have easily been enlisted into the uprising. Everyone in the audience was enrapt with the display, and no one seemed to notice as the first of the armed men began scrambling over the walls on both sides.

Hurriedly Ethoam returned to the embrace of the crowd. Below, the household guard suddenly swarmed around Jormalu and his family, submerging them in green. Ethoam assumed they meant to protect the Hierarch, but when they drew their swords, they directed them inwards. Screams burst out, and a section of the crowd surged forward.

Vendavo's chimera bridge erupted into white flames which swiftly consumed the figure of the Hierarch. At the same time the flames seemed to turn solid and crystalline so that the whole representation was swiftly encased in a transparent block. It tilted over and dropped neatly into the hole at the centre of the arena.

Now the air was filled with screams, and the entire crowd began to panic. Ethoam was knocked to the ground in the rush to escape, his head hitting the edge of a granite step.

Someone was humming tunelessly in the darkness. The air stank with all the odours of the human body, and the heat was suffocating, life-denying.

Vendavo lay on the cobbled floor, unsure of whether he had just awoken from a doze or had been half-conscious for hours. He and a host of other prisoners had been locked in the cavernous wine-cellar three days ago, fed slops by guards who would not acknowledge any of them. By day, a watery light filtered through a narrow window high in the wall at street-level, but it only turned darkness into a deep twilight so that what could be seen were huddled shadows but not recognizable human beings.

Still, there were voices, and at first some of the high-ranking prisoners had been eager to identify themselves. But Vendavo remained silent, sensing that there was safety in anonymity. Two or three times a day the guards came to the cellar and took away lords and military commanders who had been eminent under the Hierarchy. None returned.

Rumours were rife in the cellar. The Hierarchy had been overthrown, and it was said that every lord and every member of the priesthood was being executed as a matter of principle.

113

It was said that prisoners were put in stocks to be pelted by the crowd before they were tortured and their throats slit. It was said that the bodies were cut up and fed to the poor.

Vendavo listened, but he did nothing to attract attention to himself. His bones ached from sleeping on the cobbled floor, and it was only a matter of time before he came down with one of the sicknesses that were already afflicting many of the prisoners – dysentery, fevers, racking coughs. Assuming, of course, that he wasn't put out of his misery by execution first.

He drifted in and out of sleep, his dreams muddled and alarming. At length he was woken by bright lights in the cellar which made huge shadows move on the walls. A trio of guards with lanterns were wandering amongst them, calling out names and peering hard at faces as they walked roughshod over the huddled forms on the floor. Vendavo heard his own name being called.

Terror seized him. He contemplated saying nothing, pretending that he was not present. But the guards were already hauling a reluctant prisoner to his feet, ignoring his protestations. The previous day, another prisoner had resisted so fiercely he had ended up with a knife in his belly.

Unsteadily Vendavo rose and began clambering over the motionless bodies of his fellow captives, not daring to look at any of them. He identified himself to one of the guards, and was promptly ordered to stand in line with the others whose names had been called. Then they were marched up the stairs and out into a small empty courtyard. The blinding sunlight speared his eyes, and he staggered under it. He was pushed forward towards an open doorway.

Inside again, they were led along a carpeted corridor, then up several flights of stairs before being ordered to enter a small bare room with bars on its windows. Vendavo, the last in line, was about to go inside when one of the guards took his arm and said, 'You're first. Come with me.'

He was certain he would faint from hunger and wretchedness. The guard led him up more stairs, along another corridor and into a large room with a big lace-hung window at its farthest end. At a desk flanked by four more guards sat two men. One was a stranger; the other, Biru.

He rose immediately, came forward, hugged Vendavo. He

114

smelt of soap and cleanliness, was as soft and flabby as civilization itself. Vendavo caught a glimpse of his own face in a mirror on the wall, and he recoiled with shock: his hair had turned white.

'Shall we proceed?' said the man who was still seated.

Reluctantly, it seemed to Vendavo, his brother disengaged himself and returned to his seat. The other man was small, middle-aged, with thinning hair and the pinched expression of a minor cleric.

'This is Alkanere,' Biru said. 'He is the People's Arbiter.'

The title meant nothing to him, but the name was vaguely familiar. Vendavo strained to remember, then recalled the name being frequently mentioned by others in the cellar. Alkanere was the shadowy rebel leader, the very man who had masterminded the overthrow of the Hierarchy.

'Your brother speaks highly of you,' he said.

'I explained how I took you into my confidence,' Biru said hastily. 'And that you agreed to go ahead with the performance for Jormalu so that he would suspect nothing.'

Alkanere put a finger to his lips, and Biru fell silent. Vendavo saw that his brother had a gash on his forehead, a deep but already healing wound. He could not think of what to say.

'They tell me your display was impressive,' Alkanere remarked. 'Though somewhat ambiguous.'

Vendavo opened his mouth to speak, but he could summon no words.

'Fitting that the Hierarch – or at least a representation of him – should be entombed in a bridge built on the backs of our people. And how well it matched the mood of the moment.'

The moment seemed a lifetime ago, the pageant itself a distant thing, only dimly remembered. But the final flourish – yes, it was coming back to him now – had been prompted by Biru's warning. He had built it into his conception as a precaution. Would it save him?

The nets on the window were luminous with sunlight. Biru, backdropped by them, looked at once dark and faded, a dim figure with no power to speak or influence events. Alkanere leafed through some documents in front of him, turning each page slowly.

'There is no reason why we should not have you executed,'

he said matter-of-factly. 'Do you have anything to say in your favour?'

Vendavo looked at his brother, who mouthed the word: 'Speak.'

'My work has always been popular with all the people,' Vendavo heard himself saying. 'I've always given public performances, free of charge. I was raised in poverty myself. I know as well as anyone the harshness of people's lives.'

He wanted to say more, to smother the situation with words and justifications; but again some instinct made him hold back.

'Memory is one thing,' Alkanere said dryly. 'Active sympathy quite another. But let us not quibble, or delay matters longer than we must. Executing you would serve no useful purpose, whereas keeping you alive may.' He paused. 'We shall need artists who will be ready to celebrate our achievements, and we already know how capably you can rise to such a challenge. Do you understand me?'

Vendavo nodded.

'You must be prepared to serve us as well as you served the Hierarchy.'

'I'll do whatever is required of me.'

Alkanere gave him a long appraising stare before motioning to Biru.

'Take him home,' he said.

Ethoam knocked on the door and waited, huddling into his robes. Overnight it had turned cold, and a thin mist shrouded the city, presaging autumn.

It was dark behind the shuttered windows, and he was surprised when bolts began to rattle on the door. It opened.

The man was bunched up in a grubby robe, his grey-streaked hair unkempt, his expression disgruntled. Ethoam had obviously woken him.

'What is it?' he asked.

'Tilarwa. Is she here?'

The man cleared his throat and spat at Ethoam's feet.

'She's dead,' he said.

Ethoam stepped back. 'Dead?'

'She was killed in the fighting at Temple Park.'

116

The man watched him, and now there was hatred in his eyes.

'You're the priest, aren't you? That priest she was seeing.'

Ethoam wanted to say that he was no priest, but the man gave him no chance.

'Damn you all!' he shouted, and then he slammed the door in Ethoam's face.

Ethoam stood there, listening to the bolts being rammed home. He wanted to knock again, to make the man – her father, presumably – tell him what had happened. But he could not face his anger and disgust, so he turned and stumbled blindly away.

Dead. Killed in the fighting at Temple Park. And it was his fault. He had been certain she was a spy of the Hierarchy under orders to seduce him into betraying the uprising. And so, when she had come to him on the final morning, he had told her to meet him in the park, where there was to be a mass gathering before they marched on Jormalu's palace. He had never imagined that the park would indeed prove to be one of the battlegrounds in the fight for the city. Alkanere had admitted that he had not been allowed a part in the uprising because of continued doubts about his undeclared relationship with Vendavo. Various stories had circulated about the planned revolt in order to confuse Jormalu's spies, and Mersulis had kept them informed of the Hierarch's intelligence so that they could choose the least expected strategy on the day. It was ill fortune, but he was still to blame. Tilarwa was dead because he had not trusted her.

He hurried on, consumed with guilt and grief. If Tilarwa was innocent of any intrigue, then she might have been sincere in her desire to marry him. Which meant that he had betrayed not only a friend but someone who might have become far more to him. Never had he felt more contemptible.

'What are you doing on the streets?'

It was a patrol. They wore the old uniform of the Hierarchy, though now they served Alkanere and his assembly of advisors. Since the uprising, the curfew had been extended.

Ethoam reached into his robes and produced a pass. It was signed by Alkanere himself. The soldiers gave it the briefest of scrutinies before marching on.

Only now did Ethoam register his surroundings. He had reached the avenue leading down to the bridge. It was lined on both sides with gibbets on which hung those executed as traitors. There were perhaps a hundred, and every night the bodies were changed.

He began walking down the avenue, gazing over the jumble of rooftops to the dome of the temple. He had not gone near it since the uprising. Apparently Nisbisi had survived after opening its doors to the homeless and destitute. In general the priesthood had fared better than the nobility in the aftermath of the fighting, Alkanere and his assembly sparing anyone who had committed no blatant crimes. They would be needed, it was now being said, to help the people in the difficult times which lay ahead.

Ethoam averted his eyes from the corpses, with their bulging eyes and soiled leggings, their protruding tongues. Such public deaths appalled him, because they turned even the most hated enemy into a travesty that was to be pitied. He had refused to serve as an examiner in the treason inquests, even after Alkanere pronounced him eminently qualified. Judicial slaughter was just as abhorrent to him as any other kind of killing. He had always known that his commitment to the overthrow of the Hierarchy might eventually lead him to be a party to violence and death, but he never imagined it would come to such a brutal, uncompromising end.

He was a fool. A fool and a hypocrite. The air stank of death, and he was as much to blame for it as anyone else.

At the end of the avenue a line of soldiers stood on guard. Dawn had broken, but the curfew was not yet over. Ethoam paused to look back, for he had the sensation that someone was following him. But the avenue was filled only with corpses.

He showed his pass to the guards and was given permission to go on to the bridge.

The rising sun had banished the mist, and the bridge soared across the Raimus in all its splendour. It had been opened two days before, despite the original promise to the ferrymen that it would be demolished stone by stone. The assembly had decreed that it was needed to encourage trade and prosperity for everyone.

All of Vendavo's chimeras had been removed from the arena

except for the crystalline block encasing Jormalu. The figure lay face-up, its arms at its side, its eyes open. It looked quite dead. The entombment of the chimera had probably saved his brother's life. Vendavo was one of the few prisoners to be freed, and he had hastily departed the city to join his family in the quietude of their mountain retreat. His reprieve would be popular with the people, who cared nothing of his indiscretions. The Hierarch's wife, by contrast, had not survived, despite having been highly instrumental in ensuring the success of the uprising by persuading Jormalu's household guard to support the revolt. She had been killed close to where he now stood, as had Jormalu's children, whose lives she had tried to bargain for. The betrayal had not ended there, because the guard themselves were now imprisoned, awaiting a trial from which they could not expect to emerge alive.

The curfew was over, and a crowd had already started to gather at the head of the bridge. There were families with children, traders with mules, young men and widows carrying sacks and baskets, all waiting to be allowed to cross. A slim figure passed through the line of soldiers and began walking towards him. Ethoam recognized her immediately, and he felt a surge of shock and joy.

Involuntarily, he began to adjust his robes over his belly. She wore a dun-coloured linen dress, and her hair was cropped even shorter than before. As she came close, she smiled at him.

Ethoam swallowed. 'He told me you were dead.'

'I asked him to. Then I changed my mind.'

She had been allowed through the cordon without difficulty, and so presumably she had a pass just like his.

'Is he really your father?'

'Yes.'

'You followed me here.'

'Yes.'

'Why?'

'Why do you think? I wanted to see you.'

She looked even more youthful with her hair cropped, but at the same time she was very much more composed. A stranger.

'I thought you were one of Jormalu's spies.'

'No. Not his.'

He gave an empty laugh, because now he understood.

'Was it you who advised I shouldn't be trusted?'

She shook her head. 'I told them I thought your loyalty was genuine. But they preferred to take no risks. They had to be sure you kept out of mischief.'

There was an attempt at her old impudence in her expression, but he remained unmoved. She was no waif, no hot-headed temptress, or even an opportunist in the pay of the Hierarchy. It was all far more devious than that. Doubtless she had been sent to him on the final morning to keep him under scrutiny, and doubtless he had been followed throughout the day. A part of him relished the knowledge that while they had known of his visit to Vendavo, they did not suspect he had actually warned his brother. It was a small miracle the two of them had survived his indiscretion.

The guards were letting the crowd through. In a disorderly fashion they hurried forward, wheeling their carts and barrows, herding their animals, helping aged relatives along.

'Did you cut your head in the fighting?' Tilarwa asked.

'I did no fighting. I tripped.'

An old woman at the head of the crowd was pushing her handcart straight down the centre of the bridge. She ground its wheels over the block of crystal holding the chimera of Jormalu, then hurried on.

'Perhaps,' Tilarwa said, 'when things have settled down, we might meet again. Perhaps I'll come to your cubicle.'

Ethoam remained silent. He was finished with the temple, if not with his work. He intended to find a post at a retreat, caring for the sick in more sheltered surroundings. It was time to withdraw and take stock.

'Or perhaps you'll come to my house again. My father isn't such an ogre, and I owe you a proper introduction.'

'What do you want of me?' he cried. 'I've got nothing to give you.'

She looked taken aback for a moment.

'I'm very fond of you, Ethoam. I hope you believe that.'

He was still a Comforter, used to keeping his own feelings in check. He suppressed his anger and gave a smile of tolerance and forbearance. Then he pushed past her, disappearing into the tide of people which flowed in the opposite direction to the bridge's farther shore.

4

The Wailing Woman

The three-man commission arrived towards dusk, accompanied by Shubi, whom Iriyana was not expecting. Shubi had gone to Veridi-Almar two years before to study at the university, and she was now an attractive young woman of nineteen, almost a stranger to Iriyana's eyes.

Vendavo greeted her with a great display of affection, as did the ten-year-old Bila, the only one of his brood who still lived with him. Iriyana was left to usher the visitors into the reception room, where a fire blazed in the hearth and hot drinks had been provided.

She knew two of the men quite well. The eldest, Belochur, was a prominent commentator on chimera-art, while Gidrel was someone she had met at receptions in Veridi-Almar. The third, Kerkouan, was a foreigner from overseas. On their arrival, he had made a point of insisting his bags be unloaded carefully from the pack-mules. His accent was heavy but the words perfectly clear.

Belochur, renowned for his grumpiness, immediately began complaining about the chilliness of the air and the remoteness of the town itself. It was a four-day journey from the capital to the mountains, and he did not spare her any details of the indignities he had suffered while having to negotiate precipitous mountain tracks on a mule.

Presently Vendavo and his two daughters joined them for dinner. The commission had been sent to interview Vendavo about his art and to enquire about the chimeras, whose nature they were charged to elucidate. Vendavo had not wanted them to come, Iriyana knew, but he managed to deflect most of their questions by concentrating on Shubi. When the meal was over, he took both daughters away again, promising that he would submit to an interview in due course. He was contemplating a new creation, he added, and might conceivably allow them to be present at its birth.

This parting shot left Belochur both disgruntled and intrigued.

While Gidrel and Kerkouan were shown to their rooms, he lingered.

'Is this true?' he said to Iriyana. 'I understood he'd abandoned his own work and was concentrating on developing the talents of his apprentices.'

'He's never stopped creating,' Iriyana replied. 'If only as an example to his students.'

'What exactly is he contemplating?'

'That's not for me to say. Even if I could. He seldom talks about his work before it's done.'

Inwardly she was angry. Vendavo constantly talked of new projects, but they never materialized. The boast was almost certainly an empty one.

'As his agent you must be pleased he's working again.'

Iriyana shrugged. 'As I explained, he's never really stopped.'

'I can't say I cared greatly for his monument on the Raimus Bridge. Of course the craftsmanship is first-rate, as one would expect, but it has some rather vulgar elements.'

'I don't agree,' Iriyana said bluntly. 'I think it's quite remarkable.'

The monument was Vendavo's last major work in the capital, completed ten years before to celebrate the overthrow of the Hierarchy. It showed figures of every shape and variety in a pyramidal mass, clambering over one another, each striving to reach the apex of the pyramid but at the same time seeming to help one another upwards. And at the apex itself a naked figure rose out of a circle of flames, its arms beckoning to those below it. Executed as a still-life in full colour, the monument was grandiose, sentimental, even naive – but still magnificent. It dominated the centre of the bridge, and at night the flames shone with their own inner light, illuminating the androgynous figure above, a symbol of the new order, visible from almost anywhere in Veridi-Almar.

'He understands exactly why we've come?' Belochur asked.

'Vendavo? Of course.'

'You've had ample notice of our visit. The journey was most inconvenient. Especially when Vendavo regularly visits Veridi-Almar.'

'He hasn't been to the city for over a year.'

Belochur made a dismissive sound.

122

'We have other artists to interview in the city,' he said with all the pomposity he could muster. 'We can stay no more than three days.'

In the depths of the night, Iriyana surfaced from a dream of being called across a lake of moonlit water. Even as she rose out of sleep the cries transformed themselves into a series of plaintive wails which she continued to hear distantly.

She sat up. The sounds continued, growing louder. They were coming from somewhere outside, at the rear of the house.

She rose and went along the landing to a window which looked down over the orchard. A thick fog had descended and nothing could be seen. The sobbing sounds grew fainter, faded.

Iriyana turned and saw that the door to Vendavo's bedroom was open. She crossed to the doorway, peered inside. The bed had not been slept in, and there was no sign of Vendavo.

A flood of outrage enveloped her. She rushed to Shubi's bedroom, flung open the door.

'What is it?' came a sleepy voice.

Shubi was alone in the bed. She sat up drowsily, the blankets slipping down to reveal her nakedness. Her skin was eggshell pale in the dimness.

'I'm sorry,' Iriyana began, realizing her mistake. Then she heard the wailing again – long mournful sobs, drawing closer now.

'Can you hear it?'

Shubi nodded. The crease of a blanket marked her face like a scar.

'Perhaps it's a wolf,' she said. 'Or a bear.'

Iriyana shook her head. It was true that animals from the mountains sometimes prowled the gardens of the house by night, but this was no ordinary nocturnal cry. It sounded human.

Shubi reached for her nightrobe. The two of them went to the landing window. But the sounds were fading again, and the fog blanketed everything.

Shubi slipped away and returned moments later.

'Bila didn't wake,' she remarked.

All was quiet now. No one in the house had stirred apart from the two of them.

123

'Where's your father?' Iriyana asked.

'I don't know. I thought he'd gone to bed.'

Iriyana was annoyed with herself for acting so impetuously by rushing into Shubi's room. She had always suspected Vendavo of sleeping with his daughter after she reached puberty, but she was never able to broach the subject with Shubi. Though Iriyana had effectively acted as her stepmother for five years, there had always been a certain reticence between them.

'I had no idea you were coming,' she blurted.

'Father wrote, asking me to visit.'

'Oh? And did he specify a date?'

'He told me about the commission and suggested I accompany them from Veridi-Almar.'

She might have guessed as much. Shubi's visit gave Vendavo the perfect excuse for distracting himself from the attentions of Belochur and the others.

'Well,' Iriyana said more softly, 'I'm pleased you're home. You were still a girl when I said goodbye to you, but look at you now – quite the fine young woman.'

Shubi smiled. A silence fell between them – a silence which Iriyana abruptly felt was at once tense and intimate, like that between lovers.

'I'd better find your father,' she said hastily.

Next morning Iriyana found Gidrel sitting alone at the breakfast table. Through the window, she saw Shubi and Bila walking together in the orchard.

'Breakfast's in the pot,' Gidrel said.

A pan of rice was simmering on the stove; it had been flavoured with nutmeg and raisins.

'Where's Vendavo?' Gidrel asked.

'I haven't seen him this morning,' Iriyana replied. She had not seen him, in fact, since the previous evening. His bed had remained empty, and as far as she knew, he had left the house.

'Can we expect to see him today?'

Iriyana spooned rice into her bowl. 'I would hope so. Mayor Laaphre is giving a reception to welcome you this afternoon. Half the town should be there.'

She sat down opposite Gidrel with her breakfast. He let her

124

eat in silence for a while, then said, 'How long have you been his agent?'

She was certain he knew full well. She said, 'Six years.' Vendavo had appointed her almost on a whim when the regulation of artists was introduced. But she had served him well.

'What sort of man would you say he was?'

She had expected the question. 'He's wayward, careless in his dealings with others, generous, self-absorbed, a libertine. A genius at what he does.'

Gidrel lit a pipe, blue smoke shrouding his head. Tobacco was one of the many new fashions in Veridi-Almar.

'I gather his wife died soon after you arrived.'

'Two years after,' she corrected him.

'In labour wasn't it? Her and the child.'

Iriyana nodded. She had only warm memories of Nyssa, who had shown her nothing but kindness. She had given her all to the family, to bearing and raising her children, and in the end exhausted herself beyond the point of recovery.

'How did he take it?'

She swallowed a mouthful of rice, eyeing him. He seemed an odd choice for the commission because he was no authority on chimera-art. Doubtless he had been appointed because of his talent for probing the personal lives of prominent individuals. Under the Hierarchy he had been a composer of hagiographies for the recently departed ancestors of wealthy families; after its overthrow he proved himself equally adept at producing denunciations of many of his former patrons. There was no reason to think he would be well-disposed towards Vendavo.

'He was heartbroken,' Iriyana said. 'He mourned her deeply, did no work at all for at least a year afterwards.'

'You surprise me, given that he's always had mistresses.'

She wasn't going to let him anger her. 'No one could replace Nyssa in his eyes. He loved her with all his soul.'

Gidrel made a sceptical noise. 'From what I gather, you amply filled her role in the household.'

She took her empty bowl to the basin and began rinsing it out.

'If you're suggesting I became his mistress,' she said evenly, 'you're quite wrong.'

'Oh, no, I'm not suggesting that.' A placatory smile. 'Though

I'm surprised you never married.' He allowed a pause. 'The daughter, Shubi, is a pretty young thing, isn't she?'

Her cheeks flushed. She turned her back to him, ignoring the comment.

'Someone had to keep the household going while the family was in mourning,' she said. 'I was here, so I did it.'

'I wonder if his powers have failed him. He's created nothing significant for several years, isn't that true? Not since his wife's death.'

She couldn't deny it.

'It's been years since he performed for the people as he used to.'

She had to defend him. 'Public performances are very demanding. He has his family here to think of.'

'Rumour has it he spent his last visit to Veridi-Almar in the city's whorehouses.'

Straight-faced she said, 'I thought the new Arbiter had ordered all such establishments to be closed down.'

'Rumour has it he's suffering from a degenerative mental disease brought on by an overindulgence in carnal pursuits.'

How he dressed up his smears in fancy words! She laughed, thinking how loathsome he was.

'I can assure you the rumours are false. He's in full command of all his powers.'

This was said as much in hope as certainty. The truth was that since Nyssa's death Vendavo seemed to lack the capacity for solitude which was a necessary part of his art. Most of his income came from the revenues of his earlier creations.

At this point Belochur entered, grumbling that he had slept badly on a bed that was far too soft. Iriyana had never been more pleased to see him.

Mayor Laaphre had given an impressive welcoming speech, and afterwards insisted on taking his guests down into the spacious vaults of the old temple opposite his residence. The temple itself had been razed after a fire the previous summer, but the vaults survived intact and were presently home for Vendavo's thirty students. Laaphre announced that he was gathering finance for a new temple which would incorporate galleries to display

126

the works of artists with studios below ground where they could work.

Belochur, Gidrel and Kerkouan greeted this news with polite disinterest, and Iriyana, whose patience was wearing thin, welcomed their return to Laaphre's mansion for the formal banquet. The dining hall was filled with all the township's notables, including every one of Vendavo's students. The only person missing was Vendavo himself. He had not been seen all day. Iriyana had questioned his students and several of his children, but none knew where he was.

'Do you think it's going well?' Laaphre whispered across the table.

He was a relatively young man, eager to promote his township as the home of Vendavo the master and a centre of artistic excellence. The town itself was growing rapidly as an increasing flow of visitors stimulated trade, but a new temple on the scale he envisaged was certainly beyond its means at present.

'Very well,' she whispered back.

'Will Vendavo be coming?'

She shrugged, though inside she bristled. It was so typical of Vendavo to absent himself from situations he disliked and leave all the work to others.

'Are there difficulties?' Laaphre persisted.

'None that I know of.' She glanced along the table. 'Don't worry – I think our guests are being kept happy for the moment.'

Gidrel was in close conversation with Leshtu, Vendavo's eldest son, while Belochur was talking to Kumash, one of Vendavo's more promising students. They were discussing a fashionable theory that chimeras were sometimes created spontaneously, unknown to the artist, from vivid dreams or reveries; Belochur, a traditionalist, would have none of it. Kerkouan, meanwhile, was pointing at objects on the table and speaking their names in his native tongue to an attentive audience of young women.

As the meal drew to its close, various students took the floor to perform for the rest of the diners. They conjured jewelled dogs, flowers with human faces, curved mirrors that warped the diners' reflections. Finally a small volcano spewed forth all manner of fabulous creatures which promptly scuttled up

127

on to the tables before ossifying into stony mementoes of the feast.

The hall was hectic with flurries and rustlings, the invisible movement of unformed chimeras. Iriyana had been able to sense them from an early age, though she never had any desire to create herself.

Kerkouan had brought along one of his large travelling bags, and he now proceeded to unpack a variety of rods and small porcelain dishes. He assembled the rods into tall stands from which he suspended the dishes. Then he poured water into each.

While Vendavo's students continued their performance, he scrutinized each dish carefully, paying the artists themselves scarcely any attention. In response to questions, he explained that he was attempting to detect the presence of chimeras by looking for ripples in the water. He believed their manifestation should create disturbances in a liquid medium, as a wind created waves on a lake.

Belochur and Gidrel greeted the notion with derision. Iriyana herself was intrigued but sceptical. Like everyone else, she often wondered about the true nature of unformed chimeras. Were they distinct creatures inhabiting some ethereal realm or simply a mysterious aspect of the human imagination? This was one of the fundamental questions which the commission had been set up to answer, but she doubted that Kerkouan's instruments were equal to the task. While it was true that chimeras did indeed seem to cause movement in the air to those who were sensitive to them, it was never a movement that could be seen or felt in a material way. The whisperings could only be heard by not listening; the emotions that sometimes went with them could only be felt in unguarded moments.

There was a brief moment of levity when Laaphre accidentally bumped one of the dishes and Gidrel remarked that he had seen a chimera dip its toe in the water. Kerkouan finally had to admit a temporary defeat.

'The elemental presences are too weak,' he informed them, his faith in his instruments unshaken. 'I shall need Vendavo's services. They say his emanations are the most powerful, is that not so?'

By now, it was growing late, and even Laaphre had given up hope that Vendavo would appear.

'Do you think it was successful?' he asked Iriyana as they said farewell on his doorstep. 'I hope Kerkouan wasn't offended when I jarred his equipment.'

He was an unlikely mayor: gauche, earnest in his ambition, good-natured to a fault. She smiled.

'I think you've made an excellent impression.'

'Belochur looked annoyed that Vendavo didn't turn up.'

'Belochur will always find something that dissatisfies him. It's no reflection on you. Let me worry about Vendavo.'

'Perhaps something's happened to him.'

'Perhaps,' she said softly, thinking that something certainly *would* happen to him when she caught up with him.

Under a sky that blazed with stars, she climbed the hill to the house with Belochur and the others. In the city, where she had been born, the skies were never as dark or the stars as bright. She was the daughter of a minor lord, and before the uprising had organized exhibitions in public parks and squares. Chimeras always manifested themselves in a way which reflected the character of their creator, however obliquely, and her sensitivity to the creatures greatly helped her in her dealings with the artists themselves. After the uprising, which she had been lucky to survive, she decided to pursue her ambition of meeting Vendavo, the greatest artist of them all. She knew his work intimately but knew little about the man himself; she had come to the mountains with the vague intention of writing his life story. Soon after her arrival, he seduced her – or rather, she let him have her because she admired him. It was a passionless coupling, her first and last with a man. He never touched her again, and afterwards treated her with a suspicion bordering on hostility. Then Nyssa died in childbirth, and everything changed.

'I think the great Vendavo is avoiding us.'

Gidrel had come up beside her. She was in no mood to tolerate him, so she increased her pace. Gidrel, overweight and already puffing, could not keep up.

Shubi had stayed home with Bila rather than attend the feast, but it occurred to Iriyana that Bila would now be in bed. What if Vendavo had returned in the meantime?

129

With even greater haste, she ascended the path.

There was a light burning in the kitchen window. Iriyana hurried through the garden and into the house.

Shubi was in the kitchen, Bila sitting on her lap, both of them in their nightrobes. Bila was sipping warm milk from a cup.

'She couldn't sleep,' Shubi explained.

'Is your father back?' Iriyana asked.

'I haven't seen him all day. I thought he was going to the banquet.'

Iriyana felt a disproportionate relief; at the same time, her anger towards Vendavo redoubled.

Without another word, she turned and left, bustling past Gidrel and the others.

She went back down through the town, then up the other side of the valley. A half-moon had risen, lighting the stone-walled olive groves.

An old hut stood on a rocky outcrop halfway up the mountainside. Long before she reached it, Iriyana knew that Vendavo was there; she could sense the swarming chimeras which always surrounded him.

The hut had once been derelict, but it now had a new roof. Lantern light leaked out through the shutters on the window, and a thread of smoke rose up from a squat chimney.

Without announcing herself, she threw open the door.

Vendavo was in bed with Zulya, a farmer's daughter who was his current mistress. Both had been sleeping and were startled by her sudden appearance.

Iriyana did not attempt to hide her irritation.

'Is this where you've been skulking all day?'

He tried a smile: broad and generous, warm enough to melt the frostiest heart; but she was inured to it.

'I needed some time alone,' he told her.

'Alone?' she said scathingly. 'Are my eyes playing tricks with me, or isn't that a woman in bed with you?'

He made soothing motions with his hands, then reached for his robe and hastily put it on. Iriyana let him lead her outside because she did not care to conduct an argument in front of the woman.

'She's been warming my bed, that's all,' Vendavo said to her. 'Surely you'll allow me a little intimacy?'

She was actually relieved that Zulya was the object of his lust rather than Shubi, but she wouldn't let him know that.

'You disappoint me. Everyone was waiting for you at the banquet. It was disgraceful of you not to attend.'

He moved away from her, shrugged his broad back. 'I had other things to concern me.'

'Oh? Things like farmers' daughters, I presume.'

He shook his head. 'A new creation.'

She gave an exasperated sigh. But before she could speak, Vendavo reached into the pocket of his robe and thrust an object at her.

It was a brass tube, or rather two brass tubes, one inside the other, with discs of glass set into each end.

'Point it at the sky,' he said. 'Look through it.'

'What is it?'

'Look through it.'

She knew he was trying to divert her, but she was intrigued nevertheless. She raised the instrument towards her eye, but he said, 'No, the other way around.'

Under his instructions she put the narrower end to her eye and squinted. In the tiny circle of darkness at the far end there shone an uncountable number of stars.

She removed the tube, peered again, then returned it to her eye. With the instrument she could see a hundred times more stars than by her eyes alone.

'Isn't it remarkable?' Vendavo said. 'It magnifies distant things.'

He spoke with all the enthusiasm of a child. Ever since the new Arbiter in Veridi-Almar had allowed trading vessels from other lands into their ports, ships had been sailing up the Raimus and disgorging strangers from a variety of nations bearing all manner of new devices – harnesses and ploughs, eyeglasses which rectified poor vision, missiles which spat fire and rushed through the air at great speed, tiny carts and toys which could be made to move by turning a wooden key. Though his visits to the city were now infrequent, Vendavo regularly had the latest wonders transported to the mountains: lenses which concentrated the sun's light, prisms which transformed it into rainbow colours, nuggets of iron which drew nails to them without human intervention.

131

He took the instrument from her and pointed it at the moon.

'Look,' he said.

He moved his head aside so that she could put her eye to it. The moon filled the far end, and its surface was covered with markings: rugged discs and crescents, streaks and whorls, light and shade, everywhere pitted and pockmarked like a ravaged face. And yet it was beautiful, breathtaking.

Vendavo withdrew the instrument. The moon shrank to its familiar aspect, its butter-coloured surface blotched only with vague shadows.

'We live in an age of wonders,' Vendavo said grandly as the chimeras intensified their presence. 'Did you know that the sun is also marked? You can't look at it directly through the device because it blinds the eye. But the image can be displayed on a white sheet and there –'

'I take it you never had any intention of attending Laaphre's banquet?'

Vendavo was a stocky man, Iriyana only half his size. But he was in awe of her temper, and she knew it.

'I've been busy,' he said, 'readying myself for a new creation.'

'And just what sort of creation are you proposing? Or is it simply another of your evasions?'

At last he seemed to shrivel and wilt. She was constantly having to bully him, to remind him of his duties.

'Listen,' she said in a more moderate tone, 'you've been asked to assist the commission in every way you can. I know you've never liked Belochur, or Gidrel for that matter –'

'I despise them both,' he said vehemently. 'Belochur's a leech, feeding off the sweat of others. There can never be any common ground between us. As for Gidrel, he's only interested in scandal of the nastiest kind. Why should I pretend a cordiality I don't feel?'

Belochur had been regarded as the most eminent commentator on chimera-art years before Vendavo had risen to prominence. He had subsequently made many pronouncements on Vendavo's work, few of which were to the artist's liking. His consistent view was that while Vendavo's talent was undeniable, his creations lacked a serious sense of artistic purpose and a consistent moral tone.

132

Such judgements infuriated Vendavo because he considered them utterly irrelevant, as indeed he did the whole business of evaluation. 'The commentators are incapable of *liking* anything,' he had once complained to Iriyana. 'All they can do is *admire*, and always with reservations. They swallow up art whole as soon as it's produced, then spit out its bloodied bones. To them, all the sweat, all the agony of creation stands for nothing, is not even taken into account. They smother it and deaden it with their words, then move on to their next victim. Without us, they'd be nothing.'

It was rare for Vendavo to speak passionately about his art – rare, indeed, for him to discuss it in the abstract at all. Though demanding, to him it was a thoroughly natural process, something stifled by the very idea of analysis.

He squatted on the edge of the rock, pointing the instrument down at the township, which nestled in the blind end of the valley with mountains rising around it on three sides. He seemed immune to the cold.

'So,' Iriyana said, 'are you intending to hide here for the duration of their visit?'

'I'll see them tomorrow,' he said without looking up. 'I give you my word.'

She began to rage at him, to bring all her anger at his shortcomings to bear. But this time it was no use: she couldn't shame him or appeal to his fickle sense of responsibility. The overwhelming presence of the chimeras was like a cloak which shielded him from any urgency other than his own. Finally Iriyana stalked off in a huff, leaving him alone on the outcrop under the moonlit night.

Iriyana lay awake in the darkness, wondering whether Vendavo would indeed honour his promise to meet with Belochur and the others. If he did not, there would almost certainly be repercussions. In the interests of encouraging trade, the new Arbiter was eager to promote the works of chimera artists, who were unknown elsewhere, and he had appointed the commission under pressure from overseas. It was required to use the rigorous methods of investigation and analysis which were favoured by the foreigners, but Iriyana was beginning to doubt whether it would have any success in penetrating the mystery of the chimeras. Philosophers, priests and leaders in her own land had already spent uncounted centuries pondering their essence, building religions and empires out of them, slaughtering and sanctifying in their name. And still they remained elusive to human understanding.

Marooned in her bed, deserted by sleep, she felt like a sailor becalmed on a soft raft in a dark ocean. Time passed. Then she heard the sounds again.

As before, she was not at first certain she was really hearing them. But soon there was no doubt. They were the same pitiful wails which she knew no animal could produce. This time they came from the front of the house.

She slipped from bed and went to her window. Fog cloaked the garden, but lamps had been lit in the downstairs rooms, casting pools of murky light into the orchard.

The sounds grew louder – a rhythmical sobbing, sounds only a woman could make. Her breath misted the pane. She smoothed a hole in the glass, peered again.

A figure appeared.

It was a woman in a ragged stained dress. Iriyana gasped at the sight of her.

She had two heads. The second was that of a wide-eyed and hairless child. It hung on her right shoulder.

The woman sank to her knees on the sodden grass. She began rocking on her haunches, all the while sobbing so desolately it seemed that she had gone beyond hope and even self-pity. She appeared hunch-backed, and only then did Iriyana realize that the second head was attached to a body strapped to her back.

The woman was not old, but her gauntness made her look withered. Her eyes were shadowed in her thin face. The child lolled on her shoulder as she rocked; it was alive and conscious but utterly inert.

Iriyana threw on her robe and hurried downstairs. Shubi was already up, along with several of the servants.

'Fetch lanterns,' she told them, heading for the door. She heard Shubi say, 'I'm coming with you.'

Outside, everything was dank and shrouded in mist. There was no sign of the woman. Iriyana could still hear her sobbing, but distantly now, and diminishing. She hurried through the garden, the wet grass soaking into her slippers.

The sounds grew fainter. She continued to pursue them. The grounds of the house were large, bordered by dry stone walls which were tumbledown in many places. Escaping the garden would be as easy as entering it.

The cries were lost to the night.

Iriyana reached a stretch of wall. Breathless, she leaned over, putting her hands on her knees and listening while she gasped in air.

Nothing. The woman was gone.

Shubi emerged out of the mist. She, too, was panting, and there seemed to be something frantic and desperate in her expression. Iriyana reached out and hugged her.

'Did you see her?' she asked.

'No,' Shubi replied.

She leaned against Iriyana, each exhalation hot on her neck. Iriyana felt a welling of emotion which she knew was not maternal protectiveness but desire. It thrilled and shocked her all at once. Then Shubi raised her head, peering into her face with a fearless candour.

A hazy ball of light penetrated the gloom – a servant with a lantern. Shubi instantly drew back.

'Any sign of her?' Iriyana asked the servant.

He shook his head.

'Have the grounds searched thoroughly,' she told him.

She and Shubi made their way back to the house without speaking. Bila, Belochur, Gidrel and Kerkouan were all up. Every one of them had seen the woman from the windows of their rooms. Iriyana expected questions, demands, accusations, but none came.

Bila rushed to Shubi, who cuddled her. Everyone waited until the servants returned. They had found no trace of the woman.

'Was it a ghost?' Bila asked.

'No ghost,' Kerkouan said unexpectedly. 'In my room, my instruments were disturbed. It was a chimera.'

Iriyana did not sleep that night. As dawn began to break, she left the house and retraced her steps to the hut.

It was empty, the fire dead in the hearth. She stood on the outcrop, looking over the town, wondering where Vendavo might be. The sun had not yet risen over the mountaintops, and most of the townsfolk still slept. But Vendavo was an early riser.

The fog had lifted overnight, and she could see Eswarema the priestess making her portly way along the riverbank to the grain barn which was now being used as a temple. Its broad doors already hung open.

Unhurriedly, Iriyana descended the path and crossed the wooden footbridge. The barn was square, built with an arching roof which somewhat mimicked a temple's dome. Chimeras made their gentle presence felt. Iriyana slipped inside.

Benches were laid in rows on either side of the central aisle, and an altar built on trestles stood at its far end. Eswarema was burning incense and murmuring prayers. On a bench in front of her sat Vendavo, his head bowed.

Iriyana waited, listening to Eswarema's lilting, effortless drone. The priesthood had a knack of making their prayers sound hypnotic by only half-speaking the words. But Iriyana was listening carefully, and she heard Nyssa's name being called several times.

At length Eswarema stepped down from the altar. She embraced Vendavo formally and kissed his forehead.

Iriyana crept outside and sat down on the stump of an old pine until Vendavo emerged.

'I thought I might find you here,' she said gently.

Since Nyssa's death he had turned increasingly to the temple, incorporating many of its rituals into the training of his apprentices since he claimed they improved the powers of concentration and imagination. Nyssa's ashes and those of her stillborn son had been cast into the river, and Vendavo had summoned a troupe of golden angels to accompany them on their way. It was vulgar, but heartfelt. Afterwards he had come alone to her room and wept in her arms.

A flock of chimeras attended him, and she could sense a great nervousness in them, a tense, unstable energy.

'Last night we had a visitor,' she said, and then she told him about the wailing woman.

He listened in silence, gazing over her shoulder towards the river. His eyes looked red with lack of sleep, and he had a distracted air.

'Kerkouan thinks it was a chimera,' she concluded.

136

He peered at her.

'Did you create it?' she asked.

'What did the woman look like?'

'It was hard to see, because of the fog. But it wasn't Nyssa. I thought perhaps you might have made her to give Belochur and Gidrel a fright.'

He smiled at that, but did not confirm or deny it. Something told her it would be unwise to press him in his present state of mind. When she had first come to the mountains to meet him, she had imagined he would be an extraordinary person in all manner of ways. It had taken her some years to realize that he was only extraordinary with respect to his art, and there were times when even that gift seemed imposed on him, a thing given rather than earned or deserved. In every other respect he was all too fallible.

'Today,' she said, 'you promised you'd meet with Belochur and the others.'

'Later,' he said, absorbed in his thoughts. 'I'll see them later. For now, I have work to do.'

With this, he strode off towards the footbridge, pursued by his attendant host.

Iriyana sat in the reception room while a steady rain fell outside. She had arranged for Vendavo's students to visit, and Kerkouan was busy testing various contraptions while they performed for him – assemblages of springs, pulleys, levers, liquids of every variety from hot candlewax to quicksilver. The air, which stank of vapours, was busy with the movement of chimeras, while the floor gradually became more cluttered with ossifying works of art, few of which had any merit whatsoever.

Despite all the activity, an air of aimlessness prevailed. Belochur could scarcely contain his impatience, while Gidrel spent his time mocking Kerkouan's continued failure to detect the chimeras' presence. Iriyana had told them of Vendavo's promise to meet them, but the evening was drawing on, and still he had not appeared.

In the kitchen, Shubi was supervising Bila in her chopping of parsnips. She had kept the younger girl by her side all day, and Iriyana had not had any opportunity to speak with her alone. She did not know what she would say, but there was far more than words unexpressed between them.

At the moment, however, she was more preoccupied with the quiet fury which was building in her towards Vendavo. He was not only avoiding the commission but also being neglectful of his family. This had not been one of his failings before; though he often expressed disappointment that none of his children had inherited his talents, there was still a closeness between them, and they would do anything for him. Leshtu had even taken the younger children into his own household after Nyssa's death.

In the reception room, Kerkouan had abandoned his experiments and was engaged in an argument with Belochur. Iriyana quickly grasped the radical essence of it. Kerkouan believed that the chimeras themselves were solely responsible for a creation, instilling into the mind of the artist the conceit that the human imagination dictated its form, whereas in fact that form was *imposed* on the imagination by the chimeras. She now understood why Kerkouan had little interest in the artists; to him, they were simply vessels, conduits through which the creative powers flowed.

To Belochur this was both an anathema and an absurdity. Though he personally disliked most artists, he was only too ready to credit them with full responsibility for their works. Kerkouan's standpoint made the whole emphasis of his critiques meaningless, given that they were always intimately connected with the perceived strengths and weaknesses of the artists themselves.

Gidrel and most of the students had abandoned even a pretence of interest in the debate and were engaged in a game of dice. Belochur grew more irate, while Kerkouan maintained the dispassionate air of rationality for which his countrymen were renowned. At this point Kumash arrived.

The young man's dark hair was plastered to his head, and his cloak was sodden. His late arrival surprised Iriyana, because he was a serious-minded student who relished every opportunity to discuss the theory and practice of his art.

'I've come from Vendavo,' he said breathlessly. 'He's waiting for us at Laaphre's.'

The rain had petered out, and presently the moon became visible through tattered cloud. Huddled under their hooded

138

cloaks, Iriyana and the others waited outside Laaphre's mansion while Vendavo paced the expanse of waste ground where the temple had once stood.

Kerkouan had set up his stands in front of the crowd, each dish containing a different liquid. Half the town seemed to have turned out, and everyone waited with an air of expectancy. On their arrival, Vendavo had announced that he intended to undertake a major creation for their benefit. Then he instructed them to assemble outside.

Belochur muttered loudly that soon it would be too dark to see anything. But the twilight was vibrant with massed chimeras – Iriyana had never felt their presence more powerfully, more overwhelmingly. She stole a glance at Shubi, who had helped Bila up on to a wall so that she could see better. Then she felt the elemental rush of the creatures.

Where Vendavo was standing, a massive white shape began to shimmer into existence above and around him. It flickered, stabilized, flickered again, then finally settled into solidity.

Many of the watchers gave a collective gasp as the enormity of Vendavo's undertaking became apparent. It was nothing less than a great temple, fashioned of something that might have been ivory or white marble. Towers, spires and vaulted walls supported a central dome which gleamed like a diamond.

It was as big as the High Temple in Veridi-Almar, but its design owed little to any building that had preceded it. The white substance of its fabric was seamless and luminescent, the dome a many-surfaced crystal reflecting the moonlight. White steps fanned out like a river from the cavernous entrance-way. In front of them stood a pyre-dish shaped like a giant flower.

Iriyana had never seen anything like it. It was magnificent.

For long moments no one moved, as if fearful the whole structure might suddenly topple. Then a few people came tentatively forward, and others began to follow. Soon almost everyone was swarming up the steps.

The interior was equally breathtaking. In his central dome of faceted crystal, Vendavo had contrived to mimic the effect of the magnifying instrument: the whole sky was drawn closer, stars multiplied, the clouds and moon made larger. It was a dizzying effect, as if the entire dome had been thrust into the heavens.

Elsewhere, things were more placid. Curving beams and pillars created a variety of sinuous perspectives, while the high altar rose up from the floor like a wave. There were no windows; the luminous walls filled the temple with sufficient light that none were needed. Iriyana was astonished. Though she had always appreciated the magnitude of Vendavo's talent, she had never considered him capable of creation on such a scale, and by a single effort of will.

Outside, Vendavo was receiving everyone's congratulations. He looked both elated and drained. Even Belochur and Gidrel appeared impressed, though Belochur could not resist remarking that the artist had not seen fit to furnish the temple with seats for its congregation. Across the street, Kerkouan scrambled in the mud, gathering up the stands and dishes which had been overturned in the rush to inspect the temple.

Iriyana realized that for once no chimeras flocked around Vendavo. The temple had swallowed up most of the townsfolk, and a moment of silence fell. Vendavo was embracing Shubi and Bila, and Iriyana awaited her turn to congratulate him.

Then she heard the cries – the same doleful sobbing as before.

Everyone turned. From out of the night, the woman appeared.

Haggard and destitute, this time she was holding the child in her arms. Iriyana saw that it was an infant boy. His head rocked to and fro as she staggered forward with him.

Her legs were covered with mud and scratches, and her ragged dress was sodden. She was dark-haired, quite tall, and she looked like a wild animal. She began stumbling up the steps, wailing piteously. Her gaze was fixed on Vendavo.

Vendavo went rigid. Everyone else also stood motionless, too shocked by the apparition to move. The woman scrambled upwards, the child lolling in her arms, its vacant eyes a deep blue. She thrust it forward, laid it at Vendavo's feet.

He looked down at it. It was naked under a swaddle of dirty blankets, its fair hair matted to its scalp. As Vendavo made to retreat, the woman reached out and grasped the hem of his cloak. He tried to pull away, but she would not let go. Her cries were so mournful they seemed to have induced a seizure of paralysis in everyone.

Then Shubi stepped forward and scooped up the child. Kumash and Laaphre took the woman's arms and tried to lift her to her feet. Immediately she began flailing in their grasp. She burst from them, hurling herself down the steps and racing off into the night.

In the orchard, Shubi plucked a withered pear from a bough and crouched in front of the boy to show it to him. Iriyana watched from the warmth of Vendavo's study, through a thickness of glass.

The boy was pale, moon-faced, and since he answered to no name, Shubi called him Pelu, a nonsense name which she had used for her favourite doll as a child. Pelu now entirely occupied her days, even Bila being left to fend for herself. Shubi had made it plain that she had no intention of returning to the university to continue her studies.

Iriyana put the letter down in front of Vendavo.

'Who's it from?' he asked suspiciously.

'Belochur. It's about the woman.'

He said nothing, did not even pick it up. Iriyana had been hard-pressed to get him to his desk to attend to routine correspondence. He spent little time at the house now, preferring to create in the temple. The boy unnerved him, and it was not simply his stillness, his unwavering gaze. A doctor had declared the child a congenital idiot who would never be able to talk or move; but there was something else about him – an atmosphere or presence which seemed, if not malevolent, then deeply unsettling. Vendavo avoided him whenever possible.

A frost had descended overnight, and the child was bundled up with blankets in his wheelchair. Shubi was talking to him, pointing to trees, clouds, the town in the valley below. She seemed quite unconcerned by his lack of response.

Vendavo still refused to answer any questions about the boy or the wailing woman. After the woman had fled the temple, he went straight home, saying he was exhausted. Belochur and the others delayed their departure by two days in the hope of talking to him, but he would not emerge from his room. Meanwhile the woman had been found dead in an old pigsty on the outskirts of the town. A frustrated Belochur finally had

141

the body transported to Veridi-Almar for dissection before it began to spoil.

Iriyana picked up the letter. It was addressed to them both, and she had already read it.

'They still haven't identified the woman,' she said. 'But Belochur informs us that she appears perfectly human, inside as well as out.'

Vendavo rose from his desk and went over to sit by the fire. Undaunted, she continued.

'Gidrel believes the woman was a mistress of yours and the child your bastard son.'

She waited for a reaction. There was none.

'After all, the boy has your colouring. Gidrel thinks it possible the woman might have been driven mad by his idiocy and sought you out in the hope of forcing you to acknowledge his existence. He thinks she might even be someone you have no memory of seducing.'

Vendavo snorted. 'Gidrel's an idiot himself.'

He kept his back to her, squatting on the stool and staring into the flames.

'Kerkouan takes a different view. He's convinced both of them are chimeras, created quite unconsciously by you as an outpouring of grief for Nyssa's death.'

'So he's revised his opinion of artists as dumb servants of the chimeras, has he?'

'It's simply one of the possibilities he's considering, according to Belochur. And it's an interesting idea, don't you think?'

'That man is full of ideas. He's also full of nonsense.'

'So he's wrong?'

Vendavo thrust a log on the fire. 'Why should I confirm or deny anything? I owe them nothing.'

Iriyana felt renewed impatience with his evasiveness. But she had tried to browbeat him on the subject before, without success.

'Belochur would appreciate your cooperation,' she said, still scanning the letter. 'He's keeping an open mind, he says, though he's quite prepared to believe you may have deliberately created the woman and child, given that you've fashioned human specimens in the past which were perfectly lifelike. Of course, none of them were able to utter sounds,

142

but it's conceivable to him that such an advance would not be beyond your powers.'

Vendavo laughed. 'The man's a simpleton. Does he think I'll tell him if he flatters me?'

'It's more than flattery. He needs your help so that he and the others can fully discharge their duties to the Arbiter. Only you can say which of them is right.'

The flames leapt up the dark chimney. Vendavo's lips formed a smile that was not a smile.

'Does it matter to you?' he asked, turning to face her.

'I won't pretend I'm not intrigued,' she admitted. 'Also, I don't see what's to be gained by silence. What purpose does it serve?'

He did not reply. The firelight shone in his silver hair. She could feel his chimeras growing unsettled, as though confined by the room.

'If I answer you now,' he said at last, 'will you promise never to ask me about it again?'

She wanted to tell him he had no right to impose such a condition. But instead, after hesitating, she said, 'Yes.'

'Tell them I don't know. Tell them I honestly don't know.'

Then he rose and swept out of the room.

The silence which always followed his departure was profound, because his chimeras went with him, leaving not only silence but also emptiness. Iriyana laid the letter on the desk, far from convinced he had told her the truth. She was quite sure he had not consciously created the woman and the boy because he had seemed genuinely startled by their appearance. But more than that, she could not say, except that in some sense she was equally sure the boy was his. It seemed as if the woman knew him, and whether she was a cast-off mistress or an unwitting product of his most private grief, in either case the child Pelu was his creation.

Outside, Shubi was wheeling the boy back to the house. The chair had been imported from Veridi-Almar at considerable expense. The boy was perhaps three, and Iriyana had never seen him make the slightest movement.

She crept closer to the window. As she did so, Shubi looked up and saw her. Iriyana made to smile, but she noticed that the boy was also looking in her direction with his huge empty eyes.

Though nothing registered in his face, she felt he was scolding and admonishing her for an intrusion. Shubi seemed to sense it too. She leaned forward to whisper in his ear, and it was as if they were exchanging a secret which Iriyana would never be allowed to share.

Artefacts

At dawn Caro packed the children off to her mother's, then wandered around the empty house, checking that the doors and windows were locked. She lingered awhile in her husband's study, where the presence of the few remaining chimeras was strongest. They flittered unseen in the silence and shadows, forlornly seeking the mind that would never now make them discrete. They were like a whisper of wind, a movement not quite glimpsed at the corner of the eye; restless, abandoned. In a matter of days they would all be gone, and she would be left with memories and relics.

The large walled garden of the house was filled with many of her husband's creations. There were some geometrical and crystalline forms – exercises in abstract art – but most were figures: angels and lovers and dancers and waifs, a gallery of characters, once animate and gaily coloured, all now faded to drab stone.

All, that is, except Kumash's final creation, unfinished at the last. It hung in the air near the wrought-iron gate where the two guards were stationed, the fleshed-in body of a faceless man grappling with the upper half of a translucent figure, as if struggling to wrench it into existence. Kumash had worked all summer on it but had not yet brought it to life. And now it would never be finished.

A steady rain began falling as she accompanied the guards down the hillside to the town. She tugged the hood of her cloak down further, grateful for its enveloping warmth, grateful for the leather boots which kept out the mud. At least we aren't poor, she thought. At least I can retain a shred of dignity. She was glad of the guards' silence, because it made no demands on her.

The town had grown since Vendavo had made his home there almost twenty years before; she was a child then. The hostels in particular had prospered, visitors coming at all seasons to see Vendavo's chimeras newly sprung from his brow. Vendavo the genius, they called him; or more often simply the Master. A small group of newcomers were standing on the outskirts even as she passed by, watching a cluster of figures do a bravura aerial dance.

The chimeras' golden faces were radiant, their beauty and grace of movement marking them immediately as Vendavo's creations: no one else could have put such life into them. Their garments flashed in brilliant spectral hues which lit the rain-filled gloom and the rapt faces of the onlookers, who were heedless of the weather. They looked away only at the insistence of a small boy, who wandered around the crowd, prodding them with a collecting bowl into which they happily tossed coins. One of the Master's many grandchildren, no doubt.

The guards shepherded her past, and they turned down the muddy road towards Laaphre's mansion. Caro felt remote from everything, as if she were sleepwalking. The summons had come the previous night, a note pushed under the door and signed by Enthor, Laaphre's secretary. Two Inquestors had arrived from Veridi-Almar to pronounce judgement on her husband. They wished to interview her the following morning, in the mayor's residence.

Luck was with her, the rain having driven most visitors and locals alike off the streets. Laaphre, kindly to the last, had appended a handwritten note to the summons suggesting she take one of the side entrances into the mansion via an alleyway. She soon saw why: a crowd had gathered at the front. They looked restive, ill-humoured, scarcely entertained by the chimeras which gambolled and capered above their heads. Even at a distance it was plain the creations were inferior products of Vendavo's disciples; one had even been fashioned to portray him with his flowing white hair and the face of a devil-may-care sage. It attained only the status of parody.

Several of the artists wandered around the crowd, soliciting coins, but with little success. Across the street was the luminous temple where Vendavo had been murdered. The crowds were even larger there, clustered around the huge pyre-bowl containing his ashes. A fire still burned in the bowl, five days on, and the mourning continued.

A bird-like form of pastel colours was spiralling around the temple. It was not one of Vendavo's most recent creations, but it retained all its colour and vitality. Very few of his works had ossified, unlike those of lesser artists.

The guards ushered her into the mansion through a small entrance in an alleyway. Enthor was waiting in the antechamber. She could see the unease on his face the instant he caught sight of her.

'They're ready for you,' he said. 'You'd better go in.'

He spoke briskly and would not meet her eyes. This was the same man who once cornered her at a reception and told her how *marvellous* he thought Kumash's chimeras were, what a *future* he had in store.

'Am I late?' she asked. 'I set off in good time.'

'No, no. But better not keep them waiting. They've already interviewed everyone else. Go straight in.'

He indicated the double doors. Still he would not look at her. She removed her cloak unhurriedly, then waited until he was forced to take it from her. She walked past him without another word.

The hall was far bigger than she had ever imagined. During receptions it was always filled with tables, guests, the drone of conversation. At the far end, the two Inquestors were seated behind a table. Laaphre stood beside them, and he gave her a wan smile as she approached.

The elder of the two Inquestors was a stout woman of middle years; her companion was a pale young man who blinked at her from behind wire-framed glasses. Both wore the white skull-caps of their profession.

No chair had been provided for her, so she stood in front of the table. The Inquestors had a clutter of papers and documents in front of them. The woman looked severe and judgmental, the young man rather ill-at-ease. His lighter shaded blue tunic marked him as an apprentice, learning his subtle trade under the woman's guidance.

'This is Caro,' Laaphre said. 'Kumash's wife.'

'My name is Eshmei,' the woman told her formally. 'And this is Yanoyal. We're here to give a verdict on your husband's case.'

Your husband's case. A perfectly neutral and innocuous way of describing it. As if they were about to discuss some civil affair such as a dispute over property or the execution of a will.

'It was a terrible shock to her,' Laaphre began.

'Yes, yes,' said Eshmei. 'I'm sure she's quite capable of speaking for herself. You can leave us now.'

Reluctantly Laaphre withdrew, raising his hands to Caro as if to say he had done what he could. When the door closed behind him, Caro felt totally exposed before the Inquestors. Girding her defences, she decided to try to get it over with as quickly as possible.

'What do you want to know?'

Eshmei's face was set in a severe frown. She sat bolt upright in her chair.

'The most obvious question,' she said, 'is whether you believe your husband was mad.'

'Mad?'

'Not in full possession of his faculties when he committed the murder. It may have an important bearing on our verdict.'

'He wasn't mad.'

'Consider carefully. Bring your reason to bear on the question, not your emotion. The facts in the case are as clear as they can be. All that remains is the question of motive, of *culpability*. Did your husband kill Vendavo because he was deranged, or was it a premeditated act?'

'He wasn't deranged.'

Eshmei smiled, but there was no pleasantness in it. 'You surprise me. Most of the other witnesses have insisted he must have lost his reason. Perhaps they were hoping to protect you from the consequences of your husband's crime?'

'He wasn't mad,' Caro said again.

'Then in your view it was premeditated.'

'I'm not saying that, either. I'm simply saying Kumash wasn't mad.'

'If he wasn't mad, then it must have been premeditated.'

'That isn't for me to judge.'

'Isn't it? Then who is to judge, if not those who will have to live with the repercussions of his actions?'

Caro kept her face free from any expression, denying all the pain and despair she felt. Yanoyal was hunched over a ledger, diligently scribbling down her answers with a long black pencil.

'I understand that Kumash left no suicide note,' Eshmei said.

148

'No.'

'He gave you no hint of what was going to happen?'

'No.'

'I find that hard to believe.'

'It's true.'

Eshmei looked frankly sceptical. Caro knew she was one of the chief Inquestors in the capital who judged only the most heinous of crimes.

'Was he normally a violent man?' she asked.

'Never,' Caro said firmly. 'He hated violence. I never saw him even raise his hand in anger.'

'Not even to discipline the children?'

'No. He sometimes shouted at them, but that was all.'

Eshmei picked up a piece of paper without looking at it. 'We've heard from other witnesses – Mayor Laaphre included – that Kumash had been somewhat reclusive in the period leading up to the murder.'

'He had been working long hours on a new creation, putting great effort into it.'

'Would you say he was under strain?'

'That depends on what you mean by "strain". Many artists experience mental pressures to a greater or lesser degree. Often it's what helps give their work vitality.'

'Let me put it more plainly. Would you say Kumash was behaving normally before he murdered Vendavo and killed himself?'

'I saw little of him. He was engrossed in his work.'

'What sort of answer is that? You were his wife. You lived in the same house together.'

Her tone combined impatience and anger. Caro understood that there was no question of her being considered an innocent party in the murder. She shared Kumash's guilt by association.

'As far as I'm aware,' she said evenly, 'the only strain he was under was the usual one of bringing a work to life. Kumash was a quiet man. He rarely spoke of his inner feelings, even to me. I certainly had no reason to suspect he was going to kill Vendavo.'

Eshmei leafed through the papers in front of her. Yanoyal continued scribbling, his head bowed, his slender fingers pressing open the pages of the ledger.

'I'm told,' Eshmei said, 'that your husband was always devoted to Vendavo.'

'That's true.'

'He was one of Vendavo's first acolytes, was he not?'

'He wouldn't have seen it that way. "Acolyte" implies "follower", but Kumash never followed anyone. He was very jealous of the special character of his work.'

'Nevertheless, he came here as a young man with the express purpose of seeking Vendavo's patronage, is that not the case?'

'Yes.'

'And did not Vendavo take him on as an apprentice? Did he not teach him all the necessary disciplines of his art?'

'Kumash would have been the last to deny the debt he owed Vendavo. But it was a debt of *technique*, not of *form*. Vendavo taught him the mental disciplines which enabled him to materialize chimeras, but the form which they took was determined only by Kumash. His imagination remained his own.'

Eshmei gave a smirk. 'No doubt such fine artistic distinctions are of the highest importance, but here we must concentrate on more practical matters. Your loyalty to your husband is touching, and quite understandable in the circumstances. What are you trying to protect him from?'

'Nothing,' Caro said immediately. 'You want to know why he did it, but I can't help you. I don't know why.'

'Indeed? Well, we shall see. You have two young children, I gather.'

Caro nodded. 'A daughter and a son.'

'You were married six years ago.'

'Yes.'

'And Vendavo was an honoured guest at the wedding.'

'Yes.'

'They remained close friends, did they not, your husband and Vendavo, until the very end?'

'Kumash was a young man when he first came here, and his father had died when he was an infant. Vendavo was more than just a mentor to him.'

'The Master's generosity was renowned. He was always taking in waifs and strays, isn't that true? Giving anyone with the slightest talent the opportunity to learn from him?'

Caro felt a flicker of anger. But before she could say anything, Eshmei reached into one of her pockets and produced a small object which she put down on the table. It was a miniature head.

'The head was on display here at the mansion,' she said. 'Laaphre kindly let me borrow it for the purpose of this inquest. Do you recognize it?'

'Of course.'

'One of Vendavo's, I gather. Actually, the artistry is unmistakable. It was done six years ago, wasn't it?'

The perfectly formed features of her husband's face were caught in a stony material that still retained much of its colour, though the hair was greying and the blue eyes had begun to fade. She remembered it as a newly created chimera, a still-life given sufficient mass by Vendavo that it could be handled and placed on display. He had created it during the wedding reception, almost as an afterthought. Though a minor work, his genius was stamped all over it, and lesser artists would have struggled for days to fashion something with only a fraction of its qualities.

Caro had kept the head on the mantelpiece above the hearth until the visiting Laaphre, in a misguided attempt at flattery, had pretended that he thought the head was a self-portrait, Kumash's own creation. Her husband's mood had been black for days afterwards. And then the head had vanished.

'I gather,' said Eshmei, 'that this object was given to Laaphre as a gift by your husband.'

Caro nodded. 'He admired it.'

'Do you think your husband was jealous of Vendavo?'

'No.'

'Are you sure? Not in the least bit jealous?'

'No. Not in the way you think.'

'And what way would that be?'

She felt her defences crumbling. 'Everyone knew that Vendavo was the finest artist of all. Everyone knew he was the best.'

'Your husband included?'

'Kumash continually marvelled at his abilities. But he wasn't jealous in the sense that he begrudged him them.'

'In what sense then?'

151

She was floundering. 'I don't know. He didn't want Vendavo's gifts. He just wanted to be better.'

'Better?'

'Better than anyone. Not just Vendavo.'

'But Vendavo was the best.'

'Kumash was devoted to him. He always acknowledged freely the help he'd been given to perfect his own art.'

'It scarcely seems an act of devotion to stab him to death inside the temple, in full view of his apprentices.'

A renewed horror filled her, and it was difficult to keep it hidden under the functioning exterior which she had maintained for days.

The memory was almost unbearable. Summoned to the temple immediately after the murder, she arrived breathless to find Vendavo lying below the high altar – a huddled, pathetic figure in a bloodstained cream robe. His apprentices surrounded him, some weeping copiously. Kumash was sprawled at his feet, having fallen on the knife which he had used to stab Vendavo in the heart. There was a frozen expression of anguish on his face.

'He simply walked into the temple, did he not, and plunged the knife into Vendavo's chest?'

It was a moment before Caro could answer.

'So I've been told,' she said.

'While Vendavo was instructing his apprentices in the various techniques of mental focusing?'

'Yes.'

'Prior to this, he hadn't visited the temple in some months.'

Caro shook her head.

'Yes or no?'

'Not as far as I'm aware.'

'Which seems to suggest that he intended the murder and his own death to be witnessed by others.'

Caro thought about it. 'Perhaps it does.'

'Which might imply he planned the act in advance.'

'No. I don't see how you can imply that at all. It might still have been done on the spur of the moment. Kumash would have known he'd be likely to find Vendavo there.'

'Is that what you think happened?'

'I'm not saying that. But it's possible.'

152

It was strange to be discussing Kumash's behaviour in such an abstract way. But she could only contemplate it comfortably as an abstraction.

'What was your own relationship with Vendavo?' Eshmei asked.

'He was a friend of the family,' she replied.

'No more?'

'What do you mean?'

A sly smile. 'The Master's fondness for other men's wives was well known – as was his lack of scruples in enticing them into his bed.'

'*What are you trying to imply?*'

Anger was a safe emotion, and she made no attempt to hide it. But Eshmei simply waved a pudgy hand soothingly.

'I'm implying nothing. The purity of your reputation has preceded you, well attested by your friends. I was simply wondering if Vendavo ever made any advances to you.'

Caro hesitated. 'Once or twice, some years ago.'

'And you rebuffed him?'

'Yes.'

'Did Kumash know about this?'

'No. I never told him.'

Eshmei nodded sagely. 'You didn't care for Vendavo?'

'Our relationship became amicable once I made it plain that I had no intention of sleeping with him. I admired his art as much as anyone else. But he was my husband's friend, not mine.'

'I see. Then sexual jealousy could not possibly have been a motive.'

'No. There would have been nothing to be jealous of.'

Once again Eshmei leafed through the papers in front of her. Caro composed herself as best she could.

'Let us assume,' Eshmei said, 'that you really don't know why your husband killed Vendavo. Speculate. Give me your best guess.'

'That's not fair,' Caro said. 'I've told you I don't know.'

'I'm asking you to speculate. Make an informed guess on your husband's motive. Surely that's not beyond your powers?'

'No,' Caro insisted. 'I can't.'

Eshmei sighed impatiently. 'You are an intelligent woman, but do not do me the discourtesy of underestimating *my* intelligence. I'm here to get to the bottom of this, and you will stand there until you do give answers to my satisfaction.'

She waited. Caro remained silent.

'Do you fully appreciate the gravity of the situation? Vendavo was enormously popular, and there are hundreds of people in this town alone who would happily kill you for putting food on your husband's table. Kumash has deprived the world of a great artist who still had much great art to create.'

Caro would have been the last to dispute this. Ageing though he was, Vendavo had been in vigorous health and still at the height of his powers. It was a tragedy on all fronts, but a tragedy on which she couldn't allow herself to dwell. All the grief, the horror, the anger – it had to stay locked away for a while. She had to keep functioning, for the children's sake if not for anyone else's.

'Well?'

'You're asking me to pass judgement on my husband. I can't do that.'

'We can have you locked up for refusing to cooperate with this inquiry.'

'Do what you wish. The worst has already happened.'

Caro didn't know whether the threat was seriously intended, or whether her reply was itself a bluff. It was hot in the hall, and she longed to sit down. But she was certain that no chair would be provided if she asked for one.

Eshmei seemed to relent, for she began asking Caro questions about Kumash's behaviour on the day of the murder. Caro had little to tell her, but she was happier reciting facts. Kumash had risen early and locked himself in his study, as was his usual habit. She had taken the children to school. When she had returned, he was gone. Soon afterwards a messenger arrived from the temple with the news that both her husband and Vendavo were dead.

'And you still insist you had no inkling of what was going to happen?'

Caro shook her head. 'None.'

There was a pause. Once more Eshmei examined the documents in front of her, taking her time over it. The white caps made the Inquestors look both learned and skull-like, arousing both reverence and fear.

154

'May I?'

It was Yanoyal who had spoken, in a quiet, almost diffident voice. He was still huddled over the ledger, peering askance at Eshmei and adjusting his spectacles. She looked up, seemed surprised, but nodded.

'Proceed,' she said.

He blinked shyly at Caro over his glasses. She knew that, as an apprentice, his opinion on the case would carry no legal authority. Eshmei would consider his views, but she alone gave the final verdict. But he was obviously determined to play his part.

'I gather your husband didn't finish his last creation.'

'No,' she told him.

'Perhaps he despaired of creating the perfection he sought.'

'That would be more likely to make him work harder.'

'Did you love him?'

The question was unexpected, and it threw her for a moment.

'Yes,' she said. 'I did.'

'And did he love you?'

'Yes. I believe he did.'

Yanoyal made a brief note of her responses. Without looking up, he said, 'You've already told us that your husband considered Vendavo to be the best artist of all. Did he have a high regard for his own work?'

'He was a perfectionist,' Caro said. 'He would never accept second best. So he was always critical of what he produced.'

'In the early years of your marriage, he earned little from his art, and I gather that you supported the family.'

'Yes.'

'As a washer-woman.'

'Yes.'

'Did you always support his aims as an artist?'

'Always.'

'Because you loved him.'

'Yes.'

'Was he a happy man?'

Yanoyal kept his head bowed so that the top of his cap stared at her like a blank face.

'He set the highest standards for himself,' Caro said. 'That seldom leads to contentment.'

155

'But later his work became popular, critically and commercially. Didn't this make him happy?'

'It helped ease certain pressures, but it wasn't everything. Kumash was his own sternest critic. He was never completely satisfied with his work.'

'He wanted to be a great artist.'

'I've already said as much. He was an orphan, and he always claimed that becoming an artist had given meaning to his life. He wanted to leave behind something lasting.'

She saw a smile appear on Yanoyal's lips, but still he did not look up.

'He worked very hard at his art?'

'Yes. No one was more dedicated.'

'His unfinished creation – it's at the bottom of your garden, isn't it?'

'Yes.'

'I understood that Kumash normally worked in the seclusion of his study.'

'Normally, yes. But not invariably.'

Yanoyal referred to a sheet of paper. 'Yet for several days or more prior to the murder, I gather that he was again spending his time inside his study.'

'That's true.'

'Instead of completing his creation?'

Caro essayed a shrug.

'Was he producing something else?'

'Not to my knowledge.'

'Then what was he doing?'

'Sometimes, when he had difficulties with a creation, he would pause. Spend time meditating, focusing his imagination.'

'For a whole month?'

'How can I possibly know exactly what he was doing? I can't see through a locked door! What is it you want from me? I wasn't privy to my husband's innermost thoughts. He never liked to be disturbed when he was in his study, and I always tried to respect his wishes. Who can possibly know why anyone does anything in the final analysis? The only person who can tell you for certain why Kumash killed Vendavo is Kumash himself.'

Her outburst was born of fatigue and exasperation, but she did not regret it. Yanoyal, however, took it quite calmly.

'Thank you,' he said softly.

Eshmei was frowning at him, perhaps deeming his line of questioning irrelevant or impertinent. As if to stamp her authority on the proceedings once more, she began to ask Caro more questions about Kumash's activities and state of mind in the period leading up to the murder.

Caro answered as best she could, often repeating herself. Yes, Kumash had been very preoccupied with his work. Yes, he had seemed a little remote from her and the children. No, he hadn't discussed his problems with her. Yes, he had been overworking and seeing none of his friends. No, he had never previously behaved violently to herself or anyone else.

It seemed to her as if Eshmei was once again seeking evidence that Kumash had been unbalanced, and Caro wondered if she was foolish to insist he was sane. Should the murder be declared an act of madness, then there would be no penalty. But if it was deemed to be premeditated, then there would be consequences – a heavy cash fine, perhaps, or the revenues from all Kumash's works taken by the state. But she couldn't accept that Kumash had gone mad, and she had to remain true to her convictions whatever the cost.

Memories of Kumash now began to gather: she could no longer deny them. Their first meeting, he newly arrived in the town to seek Vendavo's patronage. Their courtship, a time when he had been as passionate towards her as he always was towards his art. Visits to Vendavo's house, a place crowded with finished works and thick with unseen chimeras awaiting the Master's summons. Vendavo himself, a big, hearty, generous man, conjuring brilliant chimeras while eating or drinking with his gaggle of grandchildren running around his heels and perched on his knees.

The contrast with Kumash's painstaking efforts could not have been more stark. Diligently her husband had accompanied Vendavo to the temple each morning in those early years, there to perfect his powers of concentration. Kumash had never found it easy to fashion the creatures, no matter how studiously he practised, no matter how much encouragement the ever-magnanimous Vendavo heaped upon him. 'You're the

157

best of my pupils,' the Master would tell him. 'The very best.' But that had never been enough.

She had watched him at work in the garden on his last creation. He had laboured for days to bring forth the faceless figure. Sitting cross-legged on the grass, eyes closed, he concentrated and concentrated until finally a flickering in the air heralded the slow manifestation. At length a chimera materialized – a ghostly figure, half in limbo, half in the visible world. Dusk was falling before the shape stabilized and acquired a feeble blush of colour.

And that was only the start. Kumash dissolved it, and began again the next day. Throughout summer he kept refining the creation, agonizing over its every flaw. He slept badly, woke before dawn, worked every available daylight hour. His art had never come easily; indeed, it became harder the more he struggled and failed to find that spark of genius.

Caro was always the first to be allowed to see the finished work. This was the moment she dreaded most of all. Kumash would be eager for her praise, but at the same time insistent she be brutally frank with him. He seized on the slightest hint of prevarication, was suspicious of unqualified praise, thrown into gloom by any criticism, however minor. Whatever she said, it always ended badly.

She had no answer to the problem, for brutal frankness wasn't possible. Kumash's creations were always shapely, colourful, their movements pleasing to the eye; he deserved his popularity. But he was aware, more powerfully than anyone else, that they lacked the magnificence of great art.

If only he could have accepted second best. But this had never been in his nature. And so his bitterness and frustration grew, deepening with each creation. He would tell her of the brilliant visions he held in his mind, and of how the actual manifestations inevitably failed him. Meanwhile she tended the house and raised the children. He was a considerate husband in his way, kind to all of them, often loving. But he poured so much of himself into his art that there was little left over for her and the children.

Tears brimmed in her eyes. She blinked them away. Only now did she become aware that Eshmei was no longer questioning her but had turned to Yanoyal.

'Do you have any further questions?' she asked him.

How much longer would it go on? She couldn't stand much more. To her relief, Yanoyal shook his head.

'It's time we considered our verdict,' Eshmei said to Caro. 'You will wait outside until we call you.'

Caro settled herself on the bench opposite the double doors. Enthor was nowhere to be seen – a small comfort. Since the murder, she had only felt really secure when alone.

The inquest had been the ordeal she had imagined, but she felt she had acquitted herself reasonably well. She had been loyal to Kumash while keeping her deeper feelings hidden. They were private, a matter for her alone.

But what were her deeper feelings? Only now did she realize that a sense of betrayal was uppermost. She had made endless sacrifices for the sake of Kumash's art, but he had given her little in return. His work always came first, and all her love was no substitute for it. That was what rankled – and the fact he hadn't even left her the meagre comfort of a suicide note. To the end, the distance between them remained unbridged. She and the children were simply left with his absence and a mystery that might never be solved.

Of course the Inquestors would reach a verdict, and it would be enshrined in the annals for the benefit of future historians. Ah, they would say, poring over the musty pages of Yanoyal's ledger, *that* was what happened, *that* was why Kumash killed Vendavo. As if there had to be a discrete motive, an identifiable reason. The Inquestors thought in the certainties and absolutes of their profession, as Kumash had done in his.

A door opposite the hall opened and Enthor appeared. He held a pewter tray on which was a plate of mashed vegetables and a mug of hot cordial.

'I thought you might want something,' he said hastily, putting the tray down beside her. He looked uncomfortable, his plump cheeks turning pink.

'Thank you,' she said.

He played with his hands, hesitated.

'I'm sorry,' he blurted, then hurried away.

Caro couldn't face the food, but she sipped at the cordial. Whatever happened, she would survive somehow, protect the children. Most likely she would have to leave the town, find a new place to live. A smaller house, and one without any trace of chimeras. She had never told Kumash she was also able to sense them.

Sooner than she expected, the double doors opened.

'You can come in now,' Yanoyal said softly.

Eshmei sat waiting at the table, with Laaphre standing behind her as a witness. He shook his head sadly at Caro.

Eshmei waited until Yanoyal resumed his seat. Then she referred to a sheet of paper:

'Jealousy would seem the obvious motive in this case, but many small facts point elsewhere. Whether the accused was sane or not when he committed the murder is a moot point – the sanity of anyone who murders is moot. In strict legal terms, however, the testimony of witnesses indicates that the accused, while under some strain, was not behaving abnormally prior to the murder. It also suggests that the murder was not a sudden act of passion or derangement but had been contemplated in advance and was carried out in such a way as to draw maximum attention to itself.'

Eshmei looked up from the paper. 'All the evidence regarding your husband's relationship with Vendavo indicates that he loved him and freely acknowledged his genius. But at the same time the plain fact of his murder indicates a – how shall I say it? – a *desperate* measure on Kumash's part. Something that went beyond love for any single human being.'

She paused, as if expecting some response. Caro said nothing, preparing herself for the worst.

'Kumash's work is well known in Veridi-Almar,' Eshmei went on. 'It's not as popular as Vendavo's, of course. But then your husband did not quite have his genius, did he?'

Caro remained silent. She was not required to say anything further now the inquest was over.

'I believe your husband regretted this. I believe he was aware of his limitations as an artist to a painful degree. A *desperate* degree. And his desperation grew and grew until finally he could no longer bear the idea that his work wasn't good enough. He knew he could never hope for a place in history like his master – unless. Unless he did something to ensure that his work would never be forgotten.'

How much longer would the woman talk? Why didn't she simply give the judgement?

'Do you know that your husband's creations are now more sought after in the capital than ever before? They have acquired a notoriety value – something I believe Kumash specifically intended when he murdered Vendavo. If someone knows he lacks the talent for true fame, then infamy may seem the next best option. Your husband became sufficiently unhinged with the knowledge of his limitations to see this as the only apotheosis he could hope for. His motive was not jealousy but the fanatical desire to immortalize his work.'

Silence at last. Caro was determined not to break it. Yanoyal had put the ledger aside and sat frowning into his folded hands. Caro realized he did not agree with Eshmei's analysis of Kumash's motive.

'The verdict is premeditated murder,' Eshmei announced. 'The penalty is confiscation of all property in Kumash's name and all future revenues from his chimeras. Do you have any reason to dispute these judgements?'

It was far harsher than she had imagined. Yet in some perverse martyr's way she felt it was just. All she wanted was to leave.

'No,' she said. 'None.'

'Then I see no reason why we should delay you further.'

Caro did not linger in the mansion, wanting above all to avoid Laaphre. He was the kindest of men, but kindness was precisely what she could not bear at the moment; it would crack her like an egg.

Outside the guards were gone and the alleyway was empty. She went directly home, huddling deep into her hood and keeping to the sidestreets. No one recognized her or hindered her passage. She felt relief that the inquest was over and the verdict finally given. Perhaps now she could begin to plan for a future without Kumash.

The rain had stopped and the skies were clearing as she climbed the path to the house. Entering the garden, she saw the havoc created in the short time of her absence. Kumash's chimeras had been overturned and smashed to pieces, broken limbs and heads stamped into the mud, rhombs and star crystals reduced to shards. The garden had been turned into a morass

161

by the tread of many feet – a mob, no doubt, who had perhaps fled on seeing her approach.

Only the incomplete work above the gate was untouched. It had survived because it had no solid substance and could not be damaged. Given that it hung at eye-level above the garden, Caro wondered if Kumash had ever intended to endow it with solidity or mass, though it would of course acquire both when it began to ossify, sinking slowly to earth.

Dazed, she simply stood there, not knowing what to do. Then she hurried up the path and unlocked the door.

Nothing had been disturbed inside the house. The larder was still stocked with food, and the chest holding their valuables had not been touched. At least they aren't blaming me, she thought. And then, ashamed of it, she went back outside to salvage what she could.

She was righting a small stone cupid which had miraculously survived the attack when a voice came through the gate:

'Caro? What's happened?'

It was Iriyana. Caro had not seen her since the cremation. She hurried into the garden, her cloak dragging in the mud.

'They came while I was at the inquest,' Caro told her. 'Smashed up everything they could.'

Iriyana did not bother with words of sympathy; she simply knelt beside her and began to help search through the mud for complete pieces and fragments that might be reassembled.

Sunlight and shadow flooded the garden as clouds scudded overhead. Caro watched Iriyana carefully picking broken crystals from the mud and placing them on the flagstone path. She had been both Vendavo and Kumash's agent, arranging exhibitions of their work and organizing the collection of revenues from sales.

Caro felt that she had to say something.

'I'm surprised you came. You must hate Kumash for what he did.'

Iriyana looked up. 'Caro, I'm far more concerned about you and the children at the moment.'

'It must be hard. Two of your most popular clients gone at a stroke.'

'You can't blame yourself for what Kumash did. Vendavo had a long and prolific career. His works will be earning money for

162

many years to come, and they'll live on long after we're gone. I doubt that Kumash could help himself.'

Caro began to cry. Iriyana put an arm around her shoulders until finally she stopped. Then they resumed their rooting through the mud, stacking the larger fragments against one wall.

'What happened at the inquest?' Iriyana asked at length.

'The verdict was premeditated murder. They're going to confiscate everything.'

Tears were rolling down her cheeks again. Iriyana took her into the house and sat her down in front of the hearth. She lit the fire which Caro had laid that morning, then fetched flannels and towels from the washroom. Their arms were muddied to the elbows.

'You can always appeal against the verdict,' Iriyana remarked as they washed themselves.

Caro shook her head. 'No. Enough's enough.'

Iriyana took her hands. 'Try not to worry. I'll make sure you're provided with another house. Laaphre's offered to help as well.'

'I can't ask you to do that.'

'I insist, Caro. We were friends before this happened, and we can't let it come between us now. And it isn't just charity. I've earned a good commission over the years on Kumash's work alone. It's the least I can do.'

The fire began to blaze merrily. Caro had prepared a pan of soup the previous evening, and Iriyana put it on to warm.

'Where are the children?' she asked.

'At my mother's. They'll be staying there for a few days. I thought it would be best.'

'How are they taking it?'

'I don't think either of them really understands what's happened. They haven't absorbed the fact that they're never going to see their father again.' Caro swallowed. 'In a way, it's been a small blessing, making it easier for me to cope.'

She warmed her hands at the fire. It was the first time it had been lit since Kumash's death. Like Vendavo, her husband had undergone a form of cremation: he had been thrown on to a bonfire by a mob, his chimeras shunned so that they had disappeared from the town.

Iriyana ladled out some soup.

'They claim Kumash did it to immortalize his art. To make himself notorious.'

'Then they're fools,' Iriyana said. 'That would be completely out of character, wouldn't it? He always hated sensationalism.'

'Do you think he went mad?'

Iriyana shook her head, but it wasn't a denial. 'Caro, perhaps it's better not to dwell on it now. Perhaps we'll never know.'

The room filled up with silence. Then Caro sensed the presence of a chimera – the merest hint of a rustling in the air. Quickly it was gone. She saw that Iriyana had registered it too. Neither of them spoke.

Caro emptied her bowl of soup. At length Iriyana said, 'I ought to be getting home. There's a lot to be done.'

'Of course. Thank you for helping.'

'Why don't you come with me? There's a spare bedroom you can have for the night.'

Caro shook her head. 'I'll be all right.'

'What if the mob comes back?'

'I doubt that they will. They've already had their revenge. I need some time alone.'

Iriyana did not press her. They both donned their cloaks and went down to the garden gate.

'I'll call in again tomorrow,' Iriyana said. She paused to stare at the faceless man wrestling with the phantom. 'You were lucky they couldn't destroy that one. I think it may well be Kumash's best work.'

'He was always so diligent once he started something. I still don't understand why he didn't finish it.'

Iriyana looked at her. 'You surprise me, Caro. My impression is that it *is* finished.'

Caro watched from the gate until Iriyana disappeared over the brow of the hill. Then she resumed her task of tidying the garden. Dusk was beginning to gather by the time she was finished. The rescued remains looked a pitiful sight, but she was sure that several of the chimeras could be repaired. And at least the garden no longer looked like a battlefield.

She thought of Kumash's last days – days spent sealed in his study, doing no work whatsoever. She had left food outside his door, but often it went uneaten. He was sunk in gloom, scarcely speaking to her and the children on the rare occasions when he emerged from his study. She knew he was more unhappy than ever with his work, had sensed a crisis looming. But nothing could have prepared her for the murder of the man he idolized above all, let alone his own suicide. Only now was she beginning to understand.

Iriyana had given her the clue. It seemed obvious now, and perhaps she had deliberately blinded herself to her husband's art of late, recognizing it as the source of the widening gulf between them. Kumash had made his final chimera luminous so that it would be visible by night, and already it was giving off a silvery glow. The hands of the faceless man grappling with the wraith were Kumash's own. A few nights before the murder he had cried out in his sleep: 'Damn them all!' She had assumed he was cursing the enemies he imagined he had among the commentators who criticized his work. But he hadn't meant them at all, or any other human being.

Her thoughts were interrupted by the appearance of three men. Two of them were the guards who had escorted her to the inquest. The third was a figure in blue whose glasses gleamed gold as the setting sun flashed on them.

Caro put her hands around the spears of the gate. Like a soldier behind a fortress, awaiting an attack.

Yanoyal greeted her with a nod. He was not wearing his skull-cap, and his hair was cropped to a dark stubble. He surveyed the garden without emotion.

'Iriyana informed us that a mob had destroyed your husband's creations. Mayor Laaphre insists the house is guarded tonight.'

Caro did not move or speak. The guards took up position on either side of the gate. Yanoyal studied Kumash's final chimera.

'Is this what your husband was working on?'

'Yes.'

'Remarkable,' he said, making the word sound drab.

Caro had no intention of inviting him through the gate. He adjusted his glasses on his nose. 'The bailiffs will be arriving tomorrow morning to take possession of the house. You will, of course, be allowed to retain its contents. I'm sorry it's come to this.'

'Are you?'

'Do you have other arrangements for yourself and your children?'

'We'll manage.'

He was still scrutinizing the chimera. Experimentally he raised a hand and passed it through the body of the faceless man.

'Eshmei and I will be returning to the capital tonight. Before we leave, there was one minor point I wanted to clear up – a small detail which still perplexes me.' He glanced briefly at her. 'It concerns the question of motive. Eshmei has taken the view that your husband was seeking to immortalize his work. Yet somehow I find that rather difficult to accept.'

Dark clouds were massing again, and the wind was rising. Caro clung on hard to the gate.

'I'm not here in my official capacity, of course, but merely as an interested individual. Now that the judgement has been given, nothing can alter it – short of the deceased coming back to life.' A brittle laugh. 'I simply wanted to satisfy my own curiosity.'

Still he was pretending to study the chimera, giving her only an occasional shy glance. But his shyness was deceptive, a means of disarming suspicion. The truly diffident would never have been chosen as Inquestors in the first place.

'I can't believe your husband was seeking to immortalize his art. It seems to me he was an honourable man in his way, wouldn't you agree? And you've already told us he was his own sternest critic. I don't think he had any illusions about the lasting value of his work, or any desire to invest it with a spurious fame.'

The landscape had darkened, and a heavy rain suddenly began to fall. He was looking at her directly now, all pretence of shyness gone.

'I believe he did it to immortalize himself. If he couldn't find a place in history through his own creations, then he would do so by killing someone greater than himself, become known for ever as Vendavo's murderer. *That* was the infamy he sought.'

Caro almost laughed in his face, but she managed not to reveal her incredulity. Yanoyal looked eager for her to confirm his theory. She reached over the gate and slapped him hard across the face.

166

He recoiled, staring at her with surprise.

'Yes,' she said. 'That was why he did it.'

She waited until she saw the glimmer of a smile on his bloodless lips. Then she turned and walked up the path to the house.

Rain beaded the window as she watched Yanoyal head back towards the town. Soon he was lost from sight. To come to the house in order to satisfy himself on the nuance of a verdict revealed not only an utter dedication but also a ruthless perfectionism. He would have little difficulty in becoming a master of his craft.

And yet he was wrong about Kumash, as Eshmei had been wrong. They hadn't bothered to visit the garden and inspect Kumash's final work before the inquest. Perhaps Iriyana or another witness had described it to them and they had deemed the description sufficient, the work itself not pertinent to the case. Neither had much appreciation of art, she was sure of that. Yanoyal, obsessed by his own version of the truth, had stood at the gate, missing the clue that was staring him in the face. But she had missed it, too, until Iriyana made it plain to her. Of course, no one could be certain why Kumash had killed Vendavo, but she was quite sure she understood at last. She had satisfied Yanoyal with a lie, and that was her consolation.

She banked the fire up and put the soup on to warm once more; there was enough to fill the bellies of the guards. Outside the rain poured down through the shining chimera: it grew brighter as the darkness deepened. Unlike the mobile forms which had fled the town, this one was fixed in the place of its birth, Kumash's final defiant statement.

Perhaps there was, after all, a sense in which he had been mad at the end. Certainly Eshmei was right that he had been driven by despair, and it was ironic that he probably would achieve a form of immortality through being remembered as Vendavo's murderer. But he hadn't intended that, she was sure. Ultimately he had experienced his own form of betrayal – the betrayal of his talent, the very thing which had powered him throughout his adult life. His chimeras had failed him through their imperfections, and so he had turned against them and against art in general. In his final despair, it must have seemed

167

to him that Vendavo was responsible for leading him down the path to the ultimate realization of his inadequacy. And that was why he had murdered him.

Caro opened the window and called the guards inside. The chimera's pearly glow lit the entire garden. Kumash had indeed finished it. He had left the face blank as a symbol of his alienation, and his struggle with the half-formed wraith did not represent his attempt to wrench it into existence. On the contrary, the hands were pushing, not tugging, intent on forcing the creature back into the oblivion from which it had come.

Coda

She had three servants help her carry Pelu and his chair down the icy path to the town. When the boy was settled and snugly wrapped in his blankets, she sent them back to the house.

Shubi could not remember such a winter. A huge bib of snow had collected in the cusp of the mountains above the town, driven there by the same fierce winds that had fortuitously cleared the passes so that visitors from the lowlands were able to attend the exhibition. Never had the streets been livelier, more filled with strangers. Her father's works were everywhere, many of them creations she had never seen before.

Today a warmer wind was coming from the south, promising spring. She pushed the chair through the crowds, pausing occasionally to wipe the boy's nose. Bright booths and stalls selling hot drinks and pastries had been set up all around the temple, with some of her father's earliest chimeras arranged between them as free-standing monuments. Most of them had long turned stony, and some were defaced with scrawls or daubs of mustard.

All the most important exhibits were lodged inside the temple itself, and Laaphre had proudly told her that it contained almost everything that was movable. The exhibition was being held to commemorate the tenth anniversary of her father's death. It would also help restimulate interest in the town, which had declined since her father's followers had left.

The boy began to make small whimpering noises. Shubi stopped and crouched beside him. They were the only sounds he ever made, and they usually meant he was distressed or needed something.

'What is it?' she asked, trying to follow the direction of his sapphire gaze.

She could see nothing. Perhaps the crowds were bothering him. Quickly she pushed the chair away to the outskirts of the throng.

169

The exertion made her feel light-headed, and she had to pause to regain her breath.

'Shubi,' said a voice behind her.

She turned. It was Derien, an old suitor of hers who had recently married Bila.

'How are you?' he said earnestly, each word a misty plume.

'I'm well,' she said. She had not seen him since the wedding. He and Bila had set up home further down the valley, and she lived alone now in the house with the boy.

'You're so pale,' he said. 'Have you been ill?'

She shook her head. People were always telling her she looked unwell, but it was simply tiredness.

'Bila's expecting,' Derien announced, clapping his mittened hands together.

'That was quick work.'

He looked embarrassed, which she hadn't intended.

'I'm pleased for you both.'

He stamped his feet in the snow. 'How is the boy?'

Like everyone else, he did not actually look at Pelu.

'He's well, as you can see.'

Red pimples dotted Pelu's cheeks, a sign that he was no longer a child. His eyes were fixed on Derien.

'Have you seen the exhibition?' Derien asked. Already he seemed uncomfortable, at a loss for conversation.

'Not yet,' she replied.

Pelu began whimpering again, the sounds coming from low in his throat.

'He needs attending to,' Shubi said. 'You must excuse us.'

'Of course,' Derien replied, stepping out of their path.

'Come and visit us some time,' he called as she wheeled Pelu off. 'You and the boy.'

Shubi was relieved when they were out of his sight. Of course the invitation was simply a pleasantry; neither he nor anyone else was comfortable with the boy. Some claimed he was draining the life from her, which was ridiculous. Yes, caring for him was demanding, and she couldn't remember the last night of unbroken sleep. But without her he would have died for want of attention long before now.

Under the awning of a stall, she knelt and probed under the boy's blankets. There was no wetness, no tell-tale smell. Pelu continued whimpering even more urgently than before. He was staring up at the pies and breaded rolls on the counter of the stall. The warm air was thick with the smells of cooked meat and pastry.

'Are you hungry?' she said. 'Is that it?'

His whimpering redoubled, and she knew he was.

She bought him a pastry triangle filled with minced mutton. Kneeling beside him again, breaking off pieces and feeding them into his mouth, she thought of how the authorities in Veridi-Almar had tried to take him away from her. They wanted to examine him, to probe and analyse and turn him into a specimen, a mere object for their curiosity. They thought him an utter simpleton because he couldn't speak or move; but she knew there was intelligence locked within him, and she refused to let them have him.

Flakes of pastry gathered on his chest, and she had to keep wiping his mouth. But at least he'd learned to eat, proving that his paralysis was not absolute, that he was not completely helpless.

The woman on the stall was watching both of them, fascination and disgust vying in her face. As Shubi straightened, blood rushed to her eyes, making her stagger. She glimpsed a fierceness in the boy's blue gaze moments before something lurched and a pyramid of pies fell from the edge of the counter into the snow.

The woman on the stall gave an angry cry. Hastily Shubi pushed the chair off, the woman's curses following her.

Beside a frozen well, Shubi rested. She had probably nudged the counter in her moment of dizziness, dislodging the pies. There was no reason to believe Pelu had done it. Yes, the boy was strange, and she had lost many servants who refused to stay at the house because they claimed he created night-time apparitions which terrified them; and, yes, it was occasionally true that she herself felt he possessed a kind of locked-in ability. At times, when something angered him, the air seemed to thicken as if a storm would erupt. But it was more likely that things attributed to him were simply projections of people's own fears at his strangeness. After all, no one knew whether he had been born or made. She was the only person to whom the question was unimportant.

She dusted the pastry fragments from his chest, adjusted the scarf at his neck. He seemed contented now, settled. A shiver overtook her; the wind was rising. Mustering her strength, she headed off again, deciding that it was finally time to enter the temple, where apart from anything else it would be warm.

The chair tended to slide on the snow, but she managed to control it. And the crowds parted courteously, few gawping at Pelu. She glimpsed a knot of people she knew, including one of her younger brothers; but she managed to hurry by before they saw her. It wasn't that she disliked the companionship of others, simply that the boy's presence introduced tensions she was weary of suffering.

The curved steps which radiated down from the temple's entrance posed a problem, but she was determined not to ask for help. Turning the chair around, she began to heave it upwards as gently as she could.

By the time she reached the top, blood was throbbing in her head. To her surprise, she saw that Pelu appeared to be dozing. She freed his hands from under the blankets, then wheeled him forward.

Inside, the pearly light which issued from the seamless walls emphasized the detail and colour of her father's chimeras. She moved slowly around the temple, avoiding the areas where most visitors were congregated. Practically all her father's most famous chimeras were here, from the beatific flying figures which he had fashioned just before his death to the woman Marael, who was perhaps his most notorious creation. All had lost the movement he had originally given them, and the colour was beginning to fade from Marael, who stood with her arms open as if awaiting an embrace.

The crowds were hushed, respectful. Shubi felt no emotion except a detached curiosity. She had loved her father, after a fashion, and he had loved her too, in his unique way. But these were relics of a life that had little to do with hers.

The silence was broken by a strangled sound. Shubi started, realizing that Pelu had woken.

Immediately he began whimpering fiercely. Everyone in the temple turned to look. Shubi hesitated, then rapidly began to push the chair towards the entrance.

The boy continued making his animal sounds, furiouser and

172

furiouser. It had been a risk bringing him into the temple, confronting him with her father's assembled works; he was always restless in the presence of chimera-art, especially that of her father.

She hurried out into the grey afternoon and frantically bumped the chair down the steps. She had to get him home, to the safety and solitude of the house.

Chair skittering and sliding on the snow, breaths raw in her chest, she pushed and ran, heedless of anyone in her path. The boy jerked and bounced, his lips pressed tight together, his face turning red. His cries filled her ears, obliterating everything else. She knew she should stop to try to calm him, but she was panicked – and afraid. Never had she heard him make such noises before. It was as if he had something trapped inside him, bursting to be released.

She reached the mountain path and desperately began heaving him up the hill towards the house. But her strength was fading, and it was all she could do to keep the chair upright.

A wave of dizziness made her slump to her knees. The boy's face was dark, his cries undiminished, despite the fact that mince was spurting from his lips. He appeared intent on something in the distance.

There was a roaring in Shubi's head, and the world tilted as all strength left her and she pitched forward. It seemed to her that the last thing she saw was the bib of snow detaching itself from the mountainside and dropping down toward the town like an awesome and terrifying white bird.